A Cowboy's Promise

by Debra Chapoton

book 3

in the *Hearts Unbridled* series

Copyright © 2024 by Debra Chapoton

All rights reserved.

ISBN: 9798873545346

Imprint: Independently published

Books by Debra Chapoton

Cowboy Romance:
Tangled in Fate's Reins
Rodeo Romance
A Cowboy's Promise
Heartstrings and Horseshoes
Kisses at Sundown
Montana Heaven
Montana Moments
Tamed Heart
Wrangler's Embrace
Moonlight and Spurs
Whispers on the Range

Scottish Romance
The Highlander's Secret Princess
The Highlander's English Maiden
The Highlander's Hidden Castle
The Highlander's Heart of Stone
The Highlander's Forbidden Love

Second Chance Teacher Romance series written under pen
name Marlisa Kriscott (Christian themes):

Aaron After School
Sonia's Secret Someone
Melanie's Match
School's Out
Summer School
The Spanish Tutor
A Novel Thing

Christian Fiction:
Love Contained
Sheltered

The Guardian's Diary
Exodia
Out of Exodia
Spell of the Shadow Dragon
Curse of the Winter Dragon

Young Adult Novels:
A Soul's Kiss
Edge of Escape
Exodia
Out of Exodia
Here Without A Trace
Sheltered
Spell of the Shadow Dragon
Curse of the Winter Dragon
The Girl in the Time Machine
The Guardian's Diary
The Time Bender
The Time Ender
The Time Pacer
The Time Stopper
To Die Upon a Kiss
A Fault of Graves

Children's Books:
The Secret in the Hidden Cave
Mystery's Grave
Bullies and Bears
A Tick in Time
Bigfoot Day, Ninja Night
Nick Bazebahl and Forbidden Tunnels
Nick Bazebahl and the Cartoon Tunnels
Nick Bazebahl and the Fake Witch Tunnels
Nick Bazebahl and the Mining Tunnels
Nick Bazebahl and the Red Tunnels
Nick Bazebahl and the Wormhole Tunnels
Inspirational Bible Verse Coloring Book
ABC Learn to Read Coloring Book
ABC Learn to Read Spanish Coloring Book

Stained Glass Window Coloring Book
Naughty Cat Dotted Grid Notebook
Cute Puppy Graph Paper Notebook
More children's books:

Easy Sudoku for Kids
101 Mandalas Coloring Book
150 Mandalas Coloring Book
Whimsical Cat Mandalas Coloring Book
Grandma's 5-Minute Bedtime Stories

Christian Non-fiction:
Guided Prayer Journal for Women
Crossing the Scriptures
35 Lessons from the Book of Psalms
Prayer Journal and Bible Study (general)
Prayer Journal and Bible Study in the Gospels
Teens in the Bible
Moms in the Bible
Animals in the Bible
Old Testament Lessons in the Bible
New Testament Lessons in the Bible

Non-Fiction:
Brain Power Puzzles (11 volumes)
Building a Log Home in Under a Year
200 Creative Writing Prompts
400 Creative Writing Prompts
Advanced Creative Writing Prompts
Beyond Creative Writing Prompts
300 Plus Teacher Hacks and Tips
How to Blend Families
How to Help Your Child Succeed in School
How to Teach a Foreign Language

Early Readers
The Kindness Parade, The Caring Kids: Spreading Kindness
Everywhere

Chapter 1

THE DOUBLE HORSESHOE Ranch was a picture of serenity as Thanksgiving arrived, decorated with pumpkins, gourds, corn stalks, and hay bales, but cloaked in winter white. A fresh blanket of snow had descended upon the sprawling landscapes, covering the ranch's familiar terrain in a glistening coat. Inside, the ranch house was traditionally adorned in the splendor of a Montana Thanksgiving with a decorative cornucopia filled with plastic fruits and vegetables, tiny porcelain turkeys on the mantel, and a cinnamon-spice candle emanating warmth and scent and a sense of togetherness, despite the howling wind. Outside, the season's first snowstorm promised the winter's imminent approach. Inside, there was laughter and boasting and teasing and music.

The fireplace crackled, casting a warm, flickering light that danced on the rough-hewn wooden beams above. An expansive dining table, adorned with a rich tapestry of autumn hues, groaned under the weight of the holiday spread: roasted turkey, sage-infused stuffing, mashed potatoes, and all the trimmings one would expect.

Martha, the matriarch of the ranch, bustled around the kitchen, orchestrating a feast fit for a family that extended beyond bloodlines. Dawn, the ranch's cook, and Ashley, her energetic but daydreaming helper, were busy with the last-minute things: finishing the gravy, getting the rolls out of the oven, filling the goblets. The aroma of turkey, stuffing, and pies filled the room, a delicious promise of the meal seven drooling ranch hands were about to gorge themselves on.

Jet, the new half-owner of the ranch, shared a laugh with Chase and Pete, seasoned ranch hands with hearts as big as the Montana sky. Matt, strong and dependable, leaned against the doorframe, watching the culinary whirlwind with an amused expression. Chris Thornton, with his unruly dark hair and hazel eyes, stood by the fireplace, his warm smile adding cheer to the gathering. His enthusiasm for the holiday was infectious, and his natural charisma drew everyone to him like moths to a flame. Corey, almost fully recovered from his recent accident, helped Ashley, the radiant newcomer, who had quickly become an integral part of the ranch family as well as Corey's girlfriend.

Sawyer, the quiet observer, perched by the window, a sketchpad in hand, capturing the scene in his own unique way. The room was alive with stories, laughter, and the comforting sense of family that had been cultivated during the last year.

"Okay, boys, it's time. You may take your seats." Martha moved to her usual seat and Jet held her chair for her before doing the same for Dawn.

"This looks amazing," Matt said.

Martha smiled. "Thank you. Could we all join hands for a blessing?" She waited a moment as the guys glanced at one another, a bit uncomfortable with the hand-holding, but after a couple of chuckles, they complied. "My husband used to say the longest prayers at Thanksgiving, but I know you all will start sneaking rolls if we have our eyes closed too long." She laughed. "But Chris, who has finally started coming to church with me along with Dawn, Jet, Ashley, and Corey … uh, that's a hint that the rest of you should come … has volunteered to give a short word of thanks. Chris?"

Chris cleared his throat. "Thank you, Lord, for this bounty. Amen." When Martha raised a brow at him, he shrugged his shoulders. "You said 'short' so I did short."

Corey gave a hoot as everyone dropped hands and started to grab for the nearest bowl or platter.

"Wait, wait. A toast." Jet lifted his goblet. "To our amazing cooks. Thank you, ladies. And to all our blessings."

The clinking of glasses and the joyful chatter filled the air.

"We've come a long way since last spring," Martha said, her eyes shining. "From struggles to triumphs, and a little love thrown in, we've stood together, as one big family."

Jet nodded, his gaze shifting to Dawn and Ashley. "And we've gained new family along the way. I am very grateful for this ranch."

Chris added his own opinion, his warm voice resonating in the cozy room. "Hey, this is the best place I've ever worked. Martha, you've been like a mother hen and I, for one, am thankful for that."

All the cowboys echoed the sentiment.

The wind outside howled, but couldn't compete with their laughter and conversation. The snowstorm may have buried the range in a cold embrace, but within the walls of the Double Horseshoe Ranch, the warmth of an invented family and the promise of a brighter future thawed any chill.

After the feast, as the rest of the ranch hands settled into the living room to watch football, Corey and Ashley volunteered to tackle the aftermath of dirty plates and pots and pans. With cloths in hand, they stood by the sink, washing and drying, their conversation meandering between mundane chores and meaningful dreams.

Corey looked thoughtful, putting away a stack of dishes. "You know, Ash, I'm worried about my music. I'm not sure I can play the guitar like I used to."

Ashley dried a plate and turned to him, offering reassurance. "You're incredibly talented, Corey. There are other instruments you can master with only one hand."

He raised an eyebrow. "Like what?"

"Have you considered the piano, keyboard, or even the harmonica? Well, not the harmonica. You wouldn't be able to sing. But there are countless possibilities. How about a synthesizer?" she encouraged, genuinely believing in his talent.

"Maybe you're right," Corey mused. "I have a new melody in my head. A synthesizer or maybe a keyboard would do the trick."

Encouraged by his willingness to consider the idea, Ashley continued, "And you could write lyrics. You said you have some new words for a song, right?"

A small smile played at the corner of Corey's lips. "Yeah, I do. It's been a while since I've written anything, but I'm excited about this one. It'll go with that melody line in my head, too."

"See, Corey? You're not giving up on music; everything's going to work out."

Just then, Ashley's phone beeped with a text message. She excused herself for a moment and made her way to her room, leaving Corey to finish without her. As she closed the door behind her, she dialed her friend Julia's number.

On the other end of the line, Julia's hello carried a note of panic.

"Hey, I got your text. What's going on?" Ashley asked, concerned.

Julia's voice crackled through the phone. "Ash, it's a disaster. My neighbor below me invited me to dinner and … he was deep-frying a turkey and things caught on fire. The fire department had to come. Our apartments are damaged."

"Are you okay?"

"Yeah, physically I'm fine. But I can't stay here. I need a place to stay for a while," Julia explained, her voice thick with anxiety.

Ashley's heart went out to her friend. "Don't worry, Julia. We'll figure something out. I'm sure you can stay with me at the ranch temporarily. I'll talk to Martha. Just come. Come now."

Julia's voice was filled with gratitude. "Thank you so much, Ashley. I don't know what I'd do without you."

With a promise to sort things out, Ashley hung up the phone and went to the living room. Montanans always found a way to help each other when times got tough, and the Double Horseshoe Ranch was no exception.

Matt muted the play-by-play on the TV so Ashley could explain Julia's predicament to Martha.

"Of course, she can stay here. There's one more guest bedroom. No problem."

"Thanks, Martha. I knew you'd say that. She's on her way."

Ashley went back to the kitchen to find Corey had not finished cleaning up, but he was anxious to join the guys and see how the game was going.

"Go on," Ashley said. She spent another twenty minutes scouring pots and putting the rest of the pans back in the cupboard. She turned off the overhead lights, leaving only the stove light on.

Before she walked out of the dimly lit kitchen, Ashley's phone buzzed once more, and she saw Julia's name flashing on the screen. She answered with a mix of concern and confusion, her voice carrying across the line. "Julia, where are you?"

Julia's voice held a hint of panic as she explained her situation. "Ash, I'm about a mile from the ranch, but I skidded off the road due to the snow. I'm stuck in a ditch, and it's freezing out here."

Ashley walked into the living room, her eyes darting to Corey, who was sitting on the fireplace hearth petting Martha's dog, Duke, with his good hand. She quickly summarized Julia's predicament and made it clear that someone needed to help her out.

Corey nodded in understanding. "Don't worry, I've got my new truck. I can pull her out. You stay here where it's warm. I'll get one of the guys to help."

Corey turned to Chris, who, along with everyone else, had been eavesdropping on the conversation. "Chris, are you up for an adventure? We need to rescue Ashley's friend, Julia. She's stuck in a ditch not far from here."

Chris flashed a grin, his hazel eyes filled with anticipation. "I'm in. Let's go."

As they bundled up in their warmest winter gear and made their way to Corey's truck, Corey couldn't resist a playful jab. Ashley had mentioned to him once that one of her girlfriends thought Chris was hunky. He was pretty sure it was Julia. "By the way, Chris, Julia's got a thing for cowboys

… so maybe this'll be your chance to finally snag a date with someone who doesn't eat grass and moo."

Chris snorted. "What's she like?"

"Tall, coffee-loving, twenty-something with great taste in singers."

"By singers you mean you?"

Corey scraped the windshield clear of snow. They jumped in the truck and he started it up. "Yeah, she came to one of my gigs. Honestly, she's not bad to look at."

Chris chuckled; the prospect of meeting Ashley's friend added a touch of excitement to the snowy mission. "Well, I can't fault your taste. Ashley's cute."

Their breaths formed frosty clouds in the chilled air. Corey turned the heater on.

Snowflakes danced in the chill of the night. The road was like a winter wonderland, the first big snowstorm of the season draping the landscape in pristine white.

As the tires crunched over the snow-laden road, Corey shared some more details about Julia. "So, Julia Brown is her full name. I think she's a teacher … at the high school."

Chris chuckled, picturing Julia in his mind based on the description. "Tall, coffee-loving, school Marm, and likes *your* singing? Sounds like a nut case."

"Yeah, well, if you consider those things a lack of culture, then she should be exactly your type." Corey laughed.

"Yeah, right. I don't need any help finding women."

"When was the last time you had a relationship?"

Chris gave a noncommittal grunt.

The snowfall intensified, painting the landscape in a hushed, ethereal beauty as they approached the area where

Julia was stranded. Corey spotted her car half-buried in a mound of snow by the side of the road.

They parked the truck and Corey turned to Chris and lifted his injured arm, a playful smile on his face. "Okay, cowboy, you've got the honors. Time to play the gallant rescuer."

Chris scowled, "I can't believe you're really trying to play matchmaker."

Chris pulled on his gloves and went up to the car driver's window as Corey turned the truck around and backed up as close as he dared.

Julia unrolled the window.

"Hey, I'm Chris, here to pull you out. That's Corey, your friend Ashley's guy." It took only a second to form an impression. The woman was bundled in a hat and scarf, but he could see curls of brown hair wisping out and matching the lovely brown eyes that looked up at him like a lost pup. Only no pup had ever made his heart thump extra hard like this. "Uh, put it in neutral, okay?"

"Okay, thanks." She left the window down and he walked to the back wheels and took a look.

"Hey, Corey," he yelled, "we might just be able to push it out ourselves."

"But his hand," Julia twisted her head out the window, "maybe I should push and he can drive."

Chris's mouth curled up into a smile. "Nah, you stay inside. It's getting slushy, but you're right, I don't want Corey to hurt his hand again. The kid's got talent, you know."

"I do know."

He felt a blast of warm air coming out of her window as he passed by. "I'll get a rope and we'll let the truck do the pulling."

Corey attached one end to his hitch and Chris hooked the other around Julia's car frame. He stood aside on the road and hollered instructions. A few moments later the truck had easily wrenched the car free of its trap. Chris stepped up and unhooked both ends and wound the rope as he went to Julia's window.

"All set. Do you want me to drive you the rest of the way?" He could see she might be insulted by the offer and quickly added, "I mean, unless you've been to the Double Horseshoe before, it's kind of hard to find the turn-off in the dark."

"I'd appreciate it," she said, undoing her seatbelt.

"Just a sec. I'll tell Corey."

Chapter 2

THE GUEST ROOM at the Double Horseshoe Ranch was cozy and inviting, filled with rustic charm that perfectly complemented the surrounding winter landscape. Julia settled into the room, and Ashley was there to help her get comfortable, along with Duke, who sniffed everything that came out of her suitcase.

"This is so great of you," Julia gushed. "Your boyfriend and that other guy ..."

"Chris ... as if you didn't already know his name."

"Yeah, well, he got me out of the ditch as easily as if they were roping a calf. And then he drove me the rest of the way."

As Julia unpacked, her phone beeped with a new message. "HAPPY THANKSGIVING," she read aloud, smiling at the phone.

Ashley, curious, asked, "From anyone special?"

Julia hesitated, then decided to share her tale. "Well, actually, it's from someone I've never met. We've been texting for a while now."

Ashley's interest was piqued. "Really? How did that start?"

Julia's phone buzzed with a new message. She pulled it out and chuckled. "It's from my nameless friend again," she said.

Ashley raised an eyebrow, curious. "You don't even know his name?"

Julia grinned as she tapped out a reply. "No, I don't. We've been texting since school started. He's been my go-to advice giver whenever I needed to vent about some of the unruly kids in my class."

Julia put the phone down, patted the dog, and sat down on the edge of the bed. "It's a bit of a weird story. I was struggling with a class I was teaching, so a secretary at the high school gave me the number of a retired teacher who could offer advice. I texted the number, thinking it was the teacher. It started innocently enough. I thought this former teacher could mentor me as I teach these English classes. I texted him, got some great advice, but then I found out I'd been calling the wrong number all along."

"No way. Is this guy a teacher? Is it even a guy?"

"I'm pretty sure it is. Once I told him that a kid called me Ms. Rulemaker and he answered with 'better than being Mr. Boring' so …"

"Yeah, sounds like a man, at least, and who knows, it could turn into a modern-day romance."

"If he's in Montana, maybe. It's just … different, you know? Texting someone you've never met, it's a comfortable space. And it's been surprisingly fun. It's like a pleasant addiction—we text at all hours."

"Mm-hm, but hey, there are plenty of eligible bachelors here at the ranch. I remember you showing some interest in Chris, your rescuer, at the rodeo. How was the drive here?"

Julia blushed a bit, "Oh, I was shocked when Chris showed up with Corey. It's like fate's playing with me. I was speechless when he offered to drive the rest of the way. But we didn't say much, barely anything."

Amused, Ashley leaned against the dresser, then bent down and clicked her fingers. Duke ambled over and licked her hand. She gave the old dog a thorough scratching on his neck and ears.

"Come on, let's go out to the living room and I'll present you to my ranch family. You've got a lot of names to learn."

Julia followed Ashley and Duke out the door. She left the phone on the bed, wondering if her mysterious texter would still hold her attention now that she had some real men to get to know.

The living room erupted with cheers and laughter as the football game concluded, the guys celebrating a win by their favorite team. As Ashley and Julia entered the room, the guys quickly hushed their jubilant chatter, each one jumping up to offer his seat. The television was promptly switched off, and introductions began.

Martha took the lead, introducing Julia to each cowboy, her warm smile making the newcomer feel right at home. The jovial atmosphere was infectious, and Julia couldn't help but grin as she greeted the ranch hands. And learning names was right up her alley. She usually had all her students' names learned by the third day.

As she finished, Martha directed Julia to her seat and then issued a request. "Could someone take the dog outside for his business?"

Corey, still wearing his jacket, said, "Or how about we all go outside and have a good old-fashioned snowball fight? I'll put my good arm up against anyone's."

The idea was met with enthusiastic agreement. Coats and boots were hastily retrieved, and the group, everyone except Martha, made their way outdoors, crunching through what had become good packing snow.

Snowballs flew through the crisp winter air, and laughter filled the night. Corey and Ashley found themselves locked in a playful tangle, their lips meeting in an affectionate kiss as they tumbled into a snowdrift.

Pete and Chase couldn't resist. "Looks like we have some lovebirds in our midst. Hey, that's not allowed!" Pete declared. He and Chase pelted them with a barrage of snowballs.

Chris turned to Julia. "Don't mind them; they're harmless."

Julia's heart skipped a beat at the sight of Chris's kind eyes and charming grin. Something weird happened to her: her scalp tingled, and the feeling of flakes of snow against her skin made her think for an instant that she was out here without a coat. She was mesmerized by his eyes; before, they'd been harder to see in the night, but under the porch light and the security lamps those eyes were a soft brown infused with green, as if they held the secret of autumn or spring. No words came to mind except to thank him once again for coming to her rescue earlier.

With a chuckle, Chris assured her, "No problem at all. If you're working tomorrow, I'll make sure to shovel you out so you can get to work."

"Thanks, but no need. I'm a teacher and we're off until Monday."

"Shoot, I knew that. Well, I do have to work tomorrow, snow or no snow, so, uh, see ya around." He called for the dog and Duke came. Chris opened the door and the animal went in.

"Good night, Chris, and thanks again for getting me out of that snow bank," Julia said, intending to follow Duke inside.

"And you're welcome again."

Later, in her room, Julia checked her phone for any new text messages. There weren't any so she wrote:

HEY. HOPE YOU HAD A GOOD THANKSGIVING. NOT ME. BURNT TURKEY, A MESS TO CLEAN UP, AND A HORRIBLE SNOWSTORM. IS IT SNOWING WHERE YOU ARE?

A few minutes later she got a response:

HAD A GREAT THANKSGIVING. BIG MEAL AND I DIDN'T HAVE TO DO A THING. NOT SNOWING WHERE I AM RIGHT AT THIS MOMENT. TOASTY WARM.

Chapter 3

JULIA STOOD BY the living room window, a steaming mug of coffee warming her hands as she watched the cowboys ride out on their horses, kicking up puffs of snow. Ashley and Dawn flanked her, sipping their own coffee.

With a curious tone, Julia inquired about the cowboys' early morning activities, her eyes tracking their movements in the snowy landscape beyond the window. "What are they doing out there?"

Ashley smiled, admiring the cowboys and their work ethic. "They're heading out to herd the cattle. It's something they do every day, in shifts, regardless of the weather. It's essential to keep the ranch running smoothly."

Julia marveled at their dedication. "Even in this snowstorm?"

"Especially in this snowstorm," Dawn chimed in, joining the conversation. "Cattle still need to be taken care of, no matter the weather."

A smidgeon of worry flashed across Julia's face. "But don't they need breakfast or coffee to function?"

Dawn chuckled. "Oh, they've already had their fill. They're all early risers. I already fed them and fueled them up for the morning."

Julia took another sip. "That's a relief. I wouldn't have been able to climb into the saddle, let alone ride, without my morning dose of caffeine."

"You must've been sleeping like the dead," Dawn remarked. "Those rascals were here, making a ruckus as usual. Hey, what would you like for breakfast? Eggs? Pancakes? It's my job as cook to get you fed, too."

"Try her eggs," Ashley said. "They're marvelous."

"Okay, if it's no bother, eggs would be great."

Ashley nudged her friend and the two of them followed Dawn to the kitchen. Ashley said, "While you eat, I'm going to brave the elements and go out to the barn. Martha's in the office there. I should go help her with all the calling and canceling we have to do. There won't be any riding classes today or tomorrow. I can't wait until we get that indoor arena built."

Julia laughed. "I thought only schools got snow days."

"Think of all the disappointed kids who have today off anyway," Dawn said, taking Ashley's empty cup from her.

"Believe me, the teachers love the snow days more than the kids."

Ashley grabbed her coat by the door, but before she went out, she said to Julia, "When I come back, I want to hear more about that secret admirer you have."

As soon as she was gone Dawn asked, "Secret admirer?"

"Nope, nothing like that. Ashley likes to tease. It's just that … I told her about some text messages I get from … huh, it's a long story."

Dawn turned the gas on under the pan. "I'm listening."

16

Julia gave her the same tale she'd told Ashley the night before. Then, as Julia savored the eggs Dawn had prepared, Jet strolled into the room, his boots leaving a trail of melting snowflakes behind him, his eyes set on Dawn. He was on the verge of pulling her into an embrace, but then noticed there was a guest.

"Good morning, Julia. How're you today?" Jet greeted her warmly, flashing a friendly smile.

Julia returned the smile, glad she remembered this guy's name and why he wasn't off riding with the others. "Good morning, Jet. I'm great, thank you."

Jet poured himself a cup of coffee and sat across from her at the kitchen table. "So, you're a teacher, Ashley mentioned. What's that like these days?"

Julia's face brightened at the topic. "I absolutely love it. Most of the time, it's incredibly rewarding. Of course, every class has at least one troublemaker."

Jet nodded, sipping his coffee thoughtfully. "Teaching is a noble profession. Takes a special person to guide and educate the next generation."

"Yeah, and sometimes it takes a drill sergeant or a lion-tamer. If you've got any advice …"

The conversation flowed as Julia shared her experiences and aspirations as a teacher. Jet chipped in with his own insights, drawing from his time in the military and the discipline and leadership skills he had acquired.

"You know," Jet mused, "being in the military taught me a lot about leadership and authority. Sometimes, it's about striking a balance between being stern and being com-passionate. I suppose the same thing would be true for high school kids, you know, for a teacher to know when to stand firm and when to lend an understanding ear."

Julia absorbed his wisdom, appreciating the advice from someone with diverse life experiences. "Yeah, but it's still hard. Are you in charge of the cowboys here?"

"I think the guys here look up to me, but out on the range and in general one of the other guys is in charge."

"Oh? Which one?"

"Chris Thornton. You'd think he was invisible sometimes, and then, pow, he's refereeing a fistfight in the bunkhouse and keeping it from getting serious."

As they continued chatting, Jet mentioned that he would soon be occupied with construction plans starting Monday, weather permitting. Martha had already hired a new cowboy, a drifter named Blake Broderick, to replace him in the daily ranch duties.

No sooner had he said that than a rumbling caught their attention. Dawn looked at Jet and he shrugged his shoulders, stood, and went to a window.

"Well, I'll be … Looks like the new hire has an old truck with a new blade. He's scraped a path all the way up the drive. That'll save me getting the tractor out."

"Way to make a good first impression," Dawn said.

Jet walked to the door and let Blake into the cozy ranch house. Blake was a striking figure, tall with long, dark hair and eyes that seemed to hold a mystery of their own. He stood with a certain confidence, his presence immediately capturing Julia's attention. Duke came bounding into the room, an unusual speed for the old dog, and immediately barked at the newcomer. He lunged for Blake and Jet grabbed his collar and commanded the Shepherd to stand down. The dog huffed and chuffed at Blake, but when allowed to sniff his hand he lost the hostile attitude and accepted him.

18

"Good boy, Duke. All right then ... Julia, Dawn, meet Blake Broderick, our newest cowboy," Jet introduced him with a genial smile.

"Nice to meet you, Blake," Julia said, extending her hand.

Blake removed his hat and shook her hand warmly. "Pleasure's mine, ma'am."

Dawn smiled too, "Welcome to Double Horseshoe Ranch, Blake. We're a tight-knit group here, and you'll feel right at home in no time. Just ask Julia; she's only been here since last night."

Julia nodded.

Blake glanced back and forth between them. "Thanks. I'm looking forward to being a part of the team." Blake had a slight gleam in his eyes.

Jet noticed the subtle exchange between Julia and Blake and decided to give them a moment to get acquainted. "I'll go get Martha, she'll want to meet you right away," he said, excusing himself and motioning Dawn to come with him.

With Jet and Dawn gone, Julia and Blake found themselves alone, surrounded by the comforting rustic charm of the ranch house.

Both seemed to lose the use of their tongues until Julia said, "The weather certainly seems to have taken a wintry turn." She jerked her head toward the window and the snow-laden landscape.

Blake agreed, "Yup. Quite an early snowstorm we're having. It looks like winter has pushed autumn out of the way."

"It does." Julia glanced at Blake. "Are you used to this kind of weather?"

Blake shrugged, "I've seen my fair share of snow. Grew up in Colorado, so winter's no stranger to me."

She leaned against the window frame, feeling the chill seep through the glass. "Colorado must be beautiful in the winter."

"It is. The mountains get covered in snow, everything's serene and peaceful," Blake reminisced, his eyes momentarily lost in the memories.

Julia smiled, enjoying the brief escape into his world. "Sounds magical. But Montana has its own unique beauty, too."

Blake turned to her, a roguish glint in his eyes. "I suppose you'll have to show me around to make sure I experience it properly."

Julia reddened. "Of course. We'll make sure you get the full Montana winter experience."

Chapter 4

THE RANCHHOUSE WAS alive that evening with the comforting aromas of a hearty meal being prepared. Julia stood by Dawn in the warm, bustling kitchen, engaging in a conversation that flowed as easily as the savory scents that filled the air.

"Julia, thank you for lending a hand. It's really nice of you," Dawn said as they worked on the meal for the evening.

"My pleasure. I don't know how you do it day after day. This is like another Thanksgiving feast," Julia replied, adding a heap of butter to the mashed potatoes.

"When I first got here, there were seven hungry men and it was hard at first. Now there are twelve of us including you and the new guy, so yeah, it's a lot, but it's better than working nine to five under a jerky boss … that's what I used to do."

With the storm outside gradually subsiding, the cowhands meandered in and settled around the large wooden table. Julia helped Dawn bring out the steaming dishes of roast, mashed potatoes, and vegetables, another feast fit for the hearty appetites of the ranch hands.

Corey and Jet came in behind Martha and Ashley, and all took their seats. Martha gave a blessing and everyone dug into their meal.

Over dinner, the conversation naturally drifted toward Blake's experiences and adventures. His nomadic spirit had led him across various ranches, each contributing to his diverse repertoire of skills and tales.

"Why the wandering life?" Chris asked, intrigued by Blake's story.

Blake grinned, leaning back in his chair. "Well, after high school, I had this urge to explore. See the country, one ranch at a time. I've been to Colorado, Wyoming, Idaho, North Dakota, and now here."

"Idaho?" Pete scowled. "Dang spud munchers."

Chase raised an eyebrow. "That's quite a trail you've been following. Any *other* reason for all the moving?"

Blake leaned back in his chair, his gaze fixed on Julia. "You could say I'm a restless spirit. I've always had this yearning to explore new horizons, meet new people, and learn from different places. There's a lot to see out there, and I reckon I want to experience as much of it as I can."

Julia, sitting across from Blake, smiled as he spoke. His adventurous spirit seemed the opposite of her own, making him more intriguing. His flirtatious glances added to his charm.

Chris, quietly observant, finished his dinner, folded his arms, and leaned back in his chair, his attention fully on Blake. The newcomer's tones and words had irked him. Something didn't jibe.

When dinner finished, Corey and Ashley excused themselves. "We're heading into town," Ashley explained. "Corey's got a gig at the Circle Bar, his first one since the accident."

"Yeah," Corey added, "my hand's improved faster than the doctor expected. The synthesizer wasn't working out so that was motivation to pick up the guitar again. I won't do any fancy picking, but I can strum the chords and keep on key." He laughed. "If any of y'all want to come, I'm singing at nine. First beer's on me."

As the evening wore on, Jet and Dawn diligently cleaned up the kitchen. Most of the cowboys had retreated to the bunkhouse or left for the bar, leaving only Chris and Blake in the dining room, keeping Martha and Julia company.

With seeming interest, Blake inquired about Julia's experiences as a teacher. She shared her enthusiasm for educating young minds but didn't shy away from discussing the challenges she faced.

"There are a few students who can be rather difficult," Julia admitted. "In fact, a week ago, I was so frustrated with one boy's insubordination that I was seconds from throwing my book at him."

Martha sympathized with her struggles, her voice warm and reassuring. "Isn't there someone on your staff, like an administrator, who can help you with discipline?"

Julia considered Martha's question, her brow furrowing. "Yeah, but I thought it'd be best if I handle these issues myself. Besides, there's someone I've been texting back and forth with who's been a wonderful source of support, a mentor of sorts. It's comforting to have someone to bounce ideas off."

Chris stiffened at her words. His expression shifted as he wrestled with a thought, then abruptly excused himself to go to the bunkhouse, leaving with his phone firmly in hand.

Once alone, Chris composed a text message to an unknown recipient, the words revealing his growing suspicion: JUST WONDERING IF I'VE BEEN ANY HELP TO YOU THESE LAST FEW WEEKS?

He sent the message and anxiously awaited a response that would either put his suspicions to rest or confirm the identity of the person Julia had been texting. *Could it be him?* He hadn't told anyone about the wrong number he got a few weeks ago and how addicted he'd become to talking anonymously to … whoever it was. He'd invented a fantasy woman, who now suddenly morphed in his mind into a brown-eyed brunette with a pleasant smile and smooth voice and very good grammar.

Back in the dining room as the last of the dirty plates were whisked away by Martha, a brief silence settled over the room. Taking advantage of the moment alone with Julia, Blake leaned in, his body language seductive. "So, Julia," he began with a lighthearted tone, "It seems there might be some entertaining comedy over at the Circle Bar tonight. Care to join me?"

Julia hesitated, a flicker of doubt crossing her mind. Was this an attempt to poke fun at Corey's gig? Nevertheless, she shrugged off the thought, taking the invitation at face value. "Sure, why not? A night out sounds great." Her phone pinged, but she ignored it.

They rose from their seats, donned their coats, and headed toward Blake's waiting truck, the excitement of an impromptu date tugging at the corners of Julia's lips.

As they navigated the snow-covered roads on the way to town, Blake struck up a lively conversation with her, discussing various topics, from life at the ranch to high school homecomings and proms, complimenting her if he could work it into the conversation.

Julia's phone pinged again, interrupting them. She checked the message and read one she'd missed, JUST WONDERING IF I'VE BEEN ANY HELP TO YOU THESE LAST

24

FEW WEEKS? and then a second, new message: HOPING YOU TRUST MY ADVICE.

A warm smile spread across her face as she sent a response: FUNNY, I WAS JUST TELLING SOME PEOPLE HOW WONDERFUL YOUR ADVICE HAS BEEN.

Chapter 5

THE WIND HOWLED around the ranch house, swirling the freshly fallen snow into a hypnotizing dance. Chris Thornton, bundled up in his warmest coat, trudged through the snow back toward the welcoming glow of the ranch house's windows. A grin played on his lips, a secret he could hardly contain.

Julia's warm smile and easy laughter had captured his attention from the moment they'd met. Was it only two nights ago? He'd pulled her car out of the snowy bank and driven her back; a sense of connection had settled deep within him even then though they'd spoken only a few sentences. Now, he was about to reveal a rather intoxicating surprise.

With each step, his boots crushed the powdery snow, leaving behind a trail of footprints that quickly disappeared in the wind. He chuckled to himself, marveling at how life had a way of weaving unexpected connections.

Stopping before the ranch house's entrance, Chris retrieved his phone from his back pocket. He scrolled through the messages, each one a glimpse into their worlds. Bits of their lives, interests, and dreams had been woven into their conversations along with the advice he'd offered. He chuckled at the humor they had exchanged and marveled at how they seemed to connect on so many levels.

He put a hand on the doorknob, feeling a sense of destiny at play in his life. He was convinced that some force beyond their understanding had orchestrated this meeting.

Pushing open the heavy wooden door, he called out to Martha. "Hey, Martha, it's only me!"

Her voice floated from the living room, warm and inviting. "Come on in, Chris!"

Duke padded out to sniff him, no bark necessary, and then he wandered down the hallway.

Chris entered the cozy living room, where the soft glow of the fireplace chased away the winter chill. Martha sat by the fire, a book in hand, and a steaming cup of tea on the nearby table. The room was adorned with rustic charm and the vestiges of Thanksgiving; the flickering flames cast dancing shadows on the walls. Julia wasn't there, but she had probably gone to her room for a moment. What woman could resist a crackling fire on a cold night? It didn't occur to him that Blake wasn't here anymore and he hadn't passed him or his truck outside.

As Chris settled into an armchair opposite Martha, a chuckle tried to gurgled up, but he kept it down, his heart filled with the delightful anticipation of revealing his surprise to Julia. Fate sure had an entertaining way of bringing people together, and he was eager to reveal the entertainment to Julia.

"And why are you grinning like a Cheshire cat?" Martha raised an eyebrow and brushed a few strands of gray hair out of her eyes.

"I … I have something incredibly unbelievable to tell Julia." He twisted and looked toward the hallway to the bedrooms. Duke came slowly back and curled up on his rug by the hearth.

"Oh, she's not here. Blake drove her to the Circle Bar to meet up with the others."

Chris's face fell, his expression transforming his handsome face.

"Chris!" Martha reacted. "I've seen happier looks on a neutered calf. What's wrong?"

Chris shook his head and tried to gather his thoughts.

"She went out with him? Like a date?"

Martha shrugged. "I overheard him asking her. It sounded more like two people going to the same place at the same time, er, yeah, a date."

Chris frowned, his brows pulling together in hard wrinkles. "Maybe I shouldn't say, but ..." He hesitated for a moment, chewing his lip as he debated how to proceed. Finally, he decided to be straightforward. "I've got a feeling about Blake, and it's not a good one."

Martha's brow furrowed in concern. "You've always seemed like a perceptive young man, Chris. You have good instincts where people are concerned. What seems off about him?"

Chris leaned forward, his gaze focused and intense. "You know how he gave you those recommendations from ranches he's worked at? Well, I'm not sure how much stock you put into them, but I think you should contact those ranches, Martha."

Martha considered his words carefully, her gaze distant as she thought about the decision to hire Blake. "I'll admit, I didn't reach out to them since it was Thanksgiving week. He interviewed well on the phone, and I trusted his experience.

But if you've got a gut feeling about this, Chris, it's worth looking into."

Chris nodded, relieved that Martha was taking his concerns seriously. "I just think we should make sure we know who we're bringing into our ranch family, especially with … uh, especially with the ladies who are here."

Martha patted Chris's arm reassuringly. "You're mostly concerned about Julia, aren't you? Well, I think I understand. We'll check out those references. Thanks for looking out for the ranch and its people."

Chris offered a small, appreciative smile, glad that he had voiced his concerns.

"Besides," Martha went on, "Julia will only be here a little while. Surely they'll have her apartment building back to normal by the end of the week."

Chapter 6

THE LIVELY ATMOSPHERE of the Circle Bar surrounded Julia. She and Blake sat with Matt, Chase, and Ashley at a high-top table with a good view of the stage. Wooden beams overhead held the warm glow of old-fashioned lanterns, casting a rustic charm over the place. The bar exuded the scent of aged wood and spilled drinks, blending with the lively chatter of patrons. The dim lighting created an intimate ambiance, and the stage was set for local talents to shine for the Saturday night crowd.

Corey had taken his place in the spotlight, his guitar in hand, ready to serenade the audience. The room was a sea of excited faces, eagerly anticipating the performance.

As Corey began to strum his guitar, the room hushed, and the first notes of his song filled the air. His voice was soulful, clear, and well-rehearsed. Ashley couldn't contain her enthusiasm. She leaned closer to Julia and gushed, "Isn't he amazing? I mean, seriously, my guy's got talent."

Julia smiled, enjoying the performance but also aware of the subtle attitude shift happening next to her. Blake snorted a few times in response to Ashley's praise. He drained his beer and waved a waitress over to order another. He inched closer to Julia, his gaze growing more intense. He tried to initiate a conversation despite Julia's attention to the performance.

"So, Julia," Blake began, leaning in closer, "I have to admit, I'm not much for these small-town gigs. I'm more into big-city entertainment, you know?"

Julia nodded politely, sensing a trace of arrogance in his tone. "Small-town girl here. School Marm." She laughed him off and looked back at Corey. Most patrons were listening, but many had returned to chatting and laughing.

As Corey continued to sing on the stage, Blake's advances grew bolder. He reached a hand toward Julia's shoulder, his touch lingering for longer than she was comfortable with. She looked at his hand, then caught Matt and Chase exchanging glances. She didn't know these guys very well and didn't want to give the wrong impression. She gently removed Blake's hand from her shoulder, sensing some tension coming from Matt. She tried to give him an I'm-okay look.

Blake propped an elbow closer, his voice low and suggestive. "You know, Julia, even a school teacher like you deserves a more sophisticated evening. I can show you the city lights, the real nightlife."

Julia's discomfort grew, but she managed a gracious smile. "What did you have in mind?"

"It's only an hour and a half drive to—"

Julia put a hand up to stop him. "Too far. Bad weather. I appreciate the offer, but I'm relatively content here." She cut him the meanest eye she could give, a rumbling hiss in her throat threatened to slip off her tongue and scold him verbally in her best teacher voice, but she held back.

Corey finished his song and someone in the audience requested a love song. Ashley nudged Julia and quirked her head to include the guys. "This is the song he wrote for me after his accident."

Julia tried to pay better attention to Corey, but Blake kept whispering to her or outright talking over the music.

Matt and Chase exchanged another look, this time with concern. They were both protective of Ashley, and by extension, Julia, especially given the unease radiating from her.

Corey's passionate singing filled the room again, eliciting cheers from the audience. Ashley, sitting beside Julia, was thoroughly enchanted by his performance, gushing about his musical talent. Julia smiled, appreciating her friend's excitement.

As Corey's last song came to an end, the crowd erupted into applause and hooting. Ashley joined in enthusiastically, clapping her hands. Julia did too. Blake, on the other hand, had his attention firmly fixed on Julia, his advances growing more persistent with each passing moment.

Julia shifted uncomfortably, sensing the doggedness in Blake's demeanor. "Wasn't that great? Corey's really talented."

Blake tilted in closer, his breath hot on her cheek; she felt the invasion of her personal space. "I bet I can make your time here even better." He turned his head to the side and belched.

Matt and Chase exchanged knowing glances, noticing the annoyance in Julia's expression. Ashley, watching Corey chat with admirers as he made his way back to them, remained oblivious to her friend's distress.

Julia tried to steer the conversation away, her voice firm. "Let's enjoy the next musician, Blake."

Ignoring her boundary, he persisted. "Come on, Jules, I can't help but think we could have a great time together … somewhere else. Don't be a bitch."

Her embarrassment grew, and she looked to Matt and Chase for support, silently hoping they would intervene. Matt noticed and stepped in, getting up and coming around to Blake and putting a forceful hand on his shoulder.

"I think you've had enough to drink, buddy. Maybe it's time to ease off. You seem to be roostered up and in danger of makin' the lady madder than a wet hen." Matt spoke softly, trying to defuse the situation.

Blake smirked, not appreciating the interference. "Quit your yammerin' and drink your moose drool, Matt. I'm just trying to have a friendly conversation here."

Chase joined in. "There's friendly, and then there's crossing the line. Let's keep it respectful, huh?"

The tension in the air was palpable as Blake backed off slightly, still visibly irritated. "Yeah, yeah, sorry, Jules. Wrong word choice. I need another beer."

Julia felt a mixture of relief and aggravation, hoping this encounter wouldn't escalate further.

Corey came up to the table and Ashley rose to put her arms around his neck.

"You were awesome, cowboy."

The others added their praise, all except Blake.

Chapter 7

S UNDAY MORNING BREAKFAST at the Double Horseshoe Ranch was as lazy as Duke's tail wagging. Blake sauntered into the dining room, his demeanor oozing arrogance as he surveyed the room.

"Hey, so it's true. One of the guys—that one-legged dude—said the cook takes Sundays off."

A sneer danced across his lips as he glimpsed the boxes of cereal set out for self-service. He poured himself a cup of coffee with a disdainful huff.

Sawyer and Chris had been quietly finishing their meals, absorbed in their own conversation, but Blake's comment irritated Chris. "That 'dude' is a war veteran and half-owner with Martha now."

Blake only grunted in response.

The atmosphere shifted when Julia and Ashley entered, taking seats at the table. Blake had set his cup down at one end of the table, then changed his position to sit closer to Julia.

"Julia, I had such a great time with you last night," Blake remarked with a smug grin, his words dripping with insincerity.

Chris observed them quietly, then couldn't stop himself from intervening. He spoke up, his voice calm but authoritative. "Hey, Blake, let's be polite to our guest, all right?"

Julia gave Chris what he interpreted as a grateful nod. Blake, however, gave no indication he'd back down.

He glanced at Chris with a challenging glower. "What's your problem, Thornton? I'm just trying to have a friendly chat." He grabbed one of the bowls and filled it with a sugary cereal.

"There's no problem, Broderick." Chris turned his attention to Julia, addressing her directly. "Julia, Sawyer and I were planning to attend the second service at Martha's church today. Would you like to join us?"

Sawyer gulped, "We were?"

Chris made a soft growling sound and Sawyer changed his tune. "Um, yeah, we were. Martha invites us every week. All of us ... so ... I guess you're invited, too, Blake."

Before Julia could answer, Blake rejected the idea, his demeanor growing more defiant. "Church? No thanks. I don't waste my time on that nonsense. People who do are just—"

Chris cut him off, his tone unwavering. "Julia, would *you* like to join us?" He worked to keep the irritation off his face.

Julia's eyes met Chris's, and she nodded appreciatively. "I'd love to, Chris. Thank you."

Ashley got up to get more coffee. "Was Corey awake yet?"

"Yup, he and Chase are out on the range," Sawyer answered. Sawyer glanced at Chris. "Hey, maybe I should skip church and go help them."

Chris raised an eyebrow then bobbed his head. "Sure, go ahead. Take Blake with you as soon as he finishes breakfast." He looked at Blake. "We rotate days off and since you just started, I don't have you down for a day off until Thursday. Understand?"

"Sure, boss."

***

The Sunday morning drive to the church was a picturesque journey through the snow-laden landscape. The pristine white of the snowflakes contrasted with the vibrant blue of the sky. Chris drove carefully, the tires humming softly as they navigated the snow-covered roads. Julia sat beside him, a comfortable quiescence settling over them.

Julia, looking out her window, broke the silence. "Chris, this place is stunning, especially with the fresh snow. So much prettier than in town."

He glanced at her, a small smile playing at the corners of his lips. "Yeah, it is. It's peaceful and reminds me that there's something bigger than us out there."

She nodded thoughtfully. "An apt thing to say on the way to church. Nature really advertises God's presence, doesn't it?"

"Sure does."

"So … what do you believe in? I mean, spiritually."

Chris's hazel eyes flashed and his brows went up. "That's a deep question even for a Sunday morning."

"Mm-hm, but you heard Blake start to say something derogatory about Christians, didn't you? He's obviously not a believer, but you're going to church; you must believe something."

He nodded slowly, eyes on the road. "Yup, I do. I believe in God and I believe in the value of kindness, Julia. Treating people the way you'd like to be treated. I think that's in the Bible. Golden Rule? And I believe in working hard, being true to your word."

Julia agreed, her gaze fixed on the passing scenery. "Simple yet profound. And also in the Bible, I think." She pulled out her phone and did a search. "Yup. It's one of the commandments: You shall not bear false witness against your neighbor."

He smiled. "What about you? What do you believe in?"

Julia ran a finger down the seatbelt strap, ready for the question. "I believe in the Bible. One hundred percent. But I haven't been to church in ages. Not since I left for college." She glanced at him. "Shame on me, huh?"

Chris stole a glance at her, a shade of warmth in his expression. "I think we're a lot alike."

He wanted to say more, to tell her about their weeks of texting, about how he had been her anonymous advisor, but the words eluded him. The thought danced at the edge of his mind, the secret almost spilling out. Yet, he held back, cherishing the easy banter they shared. He decided to savor the present moment, and let the day take its course.

As they arrived at the small community church, its white façade and quaint steeple welcomed them. Chris parked the truck, and they both took a moment to appreciate the serenity of the surroundings. Chris stared at the old-fashioned church. It was a simple yet charming building, nestled within the folds of nature.

With some kind of unspoken connection between them, Chris entered the church with Julia, his heart open. The warm, golden light streaming through the stained-glass windows invited them in, and the chiming bells echoed around the gathering congregants.

He sang, he worshipped, he paid attention to the sermon, but from time to time he stole glances at Julia. She had a pleasing profile, not too much make-up, nice hair … he had to force himself to get back to focusing on what the pastor was saying.

After the benediction they walked out slowly, Julia speaking to several people she seemed to know, and he nodding to a few people he recognized. He'd never thought those particular people would be church-goers, but then they might be as equally surprised to see him here.

"Good sermon," he said as he shook the pastor's hand on the way out.

"Thank you. Hey, aren't you one of Martha's cowboys out at the Double Horseshoe?"

"Yes, sir."

"Thought I recognized you from the rodeo she had there a couple of months ago. Well, we're glad to have you come to our services. You are welcome any Sunday Martha doesn't have you working the range."

Chris nodded and caught up to Julia who was hesitating at the door. The weather had changed while they were inside. The delicate snowflakes had become thick raindrops.

"You stay here," Chris said. "I'll bring the truck up under the portico and you won't have to get wet."

He rushed out, head down, and raced to the truck, nearly slipping where the pavement was slick, but he reached the truck and climbed in without getting too soaked. The first thing he did was grab his Stetson and put it back on his head. He'd felt naked without it in church. He pulled out and got in line behind several cars whose drivers—wise husbands, no doubt—were waiting their turn to pick up wives.

His phone beeped and he checked it. ARE U STILL SOMEWHERE WARM? THE WEATHER HERE JUST WENT FROM SNOW TO RAIN. UGH!

He had to laugh. Here he was with Julia and she was unknowingly texting him. There were two cars ahead of him. He had enough time to respond. I'M WARM. JUST THINKING ABOUT LUNCH. SHOULD I HAVE A BLT OR A BURGER?

The answer came in quickly: BLT, MY FAVE.

The cars ahead moved on and he pulled up. He saw Julia inside the glass doors putting her phone away. He hopped out and went around to open the door for her.

"Thanks, Chris. You didn't have to do that."

"No, ma'am, but cowboys are creatures of habit. This is what my mama taught me." He tipped his hat and gave her the grin he couldn't hold back. He almost laughed, but kept the joke to himself.

Once they left the parking lot he asked, "Mind if we stop for lunch? Dawn doesn't cook on Sundays so … my treat."

"Sure."

"I have a hankerin' for a BLT," he said, trying hard not to let his lips curl up. "Brew Haven has sandwiches and they're open on Sunday. Sound good?"

He liked the sound of her catching her breath. "Good? It sounds great. You must be a mind reader. I love BLTs."

The ambiance of Brew Haven was warm and inviting, a stark contrast to the cold and rainy weather outside. Chris and Julia settled into a corner booth, wrapped in the cozy embrace of the café. There was music coming from the overhead speaker.

Chris, smiling, said, "Hey, I like that song. You?"

"Sure."

"Got any classic tunes that make your heart sing?"

"Oh, I love classic rock! 'Hotel California' by the Eagles is a favorite. There's just something about that guitar solo that gets me every time. What about you?"

"I'm more of a country boy myself. Give me some Luke Bryan or Chris Stapleton and I'm set."

Julia nodded. "Great choices." She paused a second. "So, what do you think of the others here at the ranch? You know, the other ranch hands. I think I've got all the names straight."

"Well, you already know Pete's the practical joker of the bunch. Corey's the guitar-strumming romantic. And Sawyer, he's a joker, too, with a big heart. As for Blake ... let's just say he's still a bit of a mystery."

Julia scowled. "He's not a mystery to me. He's a jerk, plain and simple."

Chris raised an eyebrow. "Why do you say that? Weren't you out with him last night?"

"I was, and that won't happen again."

They said nothing as the waitress brought them their sandwiches. Once the waitress left, Julia said, "You know, I'm new to this ranch life living. I grew up in a small town, the oldest of three kids. My parents worked long hours, and I had to look out for my younger siblings, helped them with homework. I didn't mind it, though. It taught me responsibility and the importance of family. And that's probably the reason I like giving homework." She chuckled and took a bite. "Mm, this BLT is awesome."

"It is."

"Your turn. What about your family?"

Chris swallowed. "Growing up, my family had this old ranch just outside of Billings. We didn't have much, but we had each other. I was happy."

"Sounds nice."

Their conversation continued to flow effortlessly, and they shared laughter, light and flirty. They even discussed the pastor's sermon. The spark between them was undeniable, like an electric current that energized the air. Julia's eyes sparkled as she spoke, and Chris found himself drawn to her infectious energy. They exchanged more stories, sharing bits of their lives, and found a surprising number of common interests.

As they finished their BLT sandwiches and sipped their coffees, a bad feeling fell over Chris. He glanced up, his expression turning somber, his features hardening. Blake had entered the café, his eyes scanning the room until they locked onto Julia.

Julia frowned, sensing the shift in the atmosphere. "Chris, is everything okay?"

Blake approached their table, a sly smile playing on his lips. "Well, well, isn't this cozy?"

Chris stood up, his eyes narrowing. "Blake, you're supposed to be out on the range. What are you doing here?"

Blake shrugged, feigning innocence. "Pete sent me out for coffee. I'm just grabbing a cup."

Chris saw through the lie, the frustration boiling beneath the surface. He excused himself from Julia and led Blake outside, the wind biting into their skin as the rain continued to fall.

"What's going on, Blake? We can't have you slacking off," Chris warned, his voice tense.

Blake chuckled, taunting. "What's it to you, Chris? Feeling threatened by some healthy competition?"

"Competition?"

"Yeah, with the ladies, er, with *that* lady."

"Listen," Chris said, his voice low and menacing, "I don't know what your game is, but you'd better get your act together. Julia's here as our guest, and I won't tolerate any nonsense."

"*You* won't? You're not my boss. What're you gonna do? *Tattle*?"

"Just get back to work."

Blake's expression wavered. He stared a moment longer at Chris, glanced through the window, then said, "Sure, man. No problem."

He turned on his heel and walked off. Chris watched as he left, his steps unhurried, no coffee to go. He returned to the booth where Julia waited, her eyes filled with concern.

"Chris, I don't think that was a coincidence. He might have been following us or rather me."

Chris nodded, his protective instincts flaring. "We'll keep an eye out. Meanwhile, do you want to go check on your apartment? See if they've made any progress in fixing the smoke and fire damage?"

She agreed and he paid the bill, leaving a large tip on the table.

Julia directed him to her apartment, where she couldn't even get in. The damage was extensive, and she'd have to prolong her temporary stay at the ranch.

"Thank goodness I'd left my school things in my car last Wednesday," she said. "I'll be spending the rest of this afternoon correcting papers … but … I love teaching."

"Sounds like teaching has a 24/7 schedule, kind of like ranching. I'll be out in the barn as soon as we get back."

He drove her back to the ranch and she thanked him again for taking her to church.

Chapter 8

JULIA KNOCKED LIGHTLY on Ashley's bedroom door, pushing it open when she heard a convivial response. The room was warm and inviting, just like Ashley herself.

"Hey there," Julia greeted, stepping into the room. "Can we chat for a bit?"

"Of course," Ashley replied, patting the empty space beside her on the bed. "I just got off the phone with Emma. She and Megan heard about your apartment fire and were wondering how you are."

"I'll give them each a call later."

"Okay … so what's on your mind?"

Julia perched on the edge of the bed and took a deep breath. "So, I need to tell you what happened this morning. You won't believe how weird it was … and I'm beginning to think Chris makes a pretty good guardian angel."

Ashley drew her legs up and put her arms around them. "Yeah, he's one of my favorites here … after Corey, of course."

"He invited me to church with him and Sawyer, but Sawyer ended up not going so it was only us two," Julia explained, her excitement starting to show. "He looked so

43

handsome. All clean shaven, clean Levi's, and a crisp white shirt. Not plaid." She gave a little hum of approval. "He kept opening doors for me and keeping me out of the rain by driving up to the portico."

Ashley grinned, obviously thrilled by Julia's animation. "Wow, that's so sweet! Chris is definitely a thoroughbred."

"Yeah," Julia said dreamily, "and he has this way of being flirty and serious all at once. It's enthralling."

Ashley nudged her playfully. "Sounds like someone's got a crush!"

Julia blushed, looking down at her hands. "Maybe a little. I mean, he's just ... really great, you know? And I'm so ready. And he took me to lunch afterward at Brew Haven."

Ashley leaned closer, her voice softening. "I get it. Chris is amazing. Just don't let him know you're texting with a stranger."

"Never. I feel kind of weird about that. Like maybe I should get the guy's name ... or block his number."

"Oh, you don't have to do that. It's not like he's a stalker."

Ashley drew in a breath. "Speaking of stalkers ... that's why I said something weird happened this morning. It was Blake ... he has me all edgy. He showed up at the café, too, like he was following me."

Ashley frowned. "We don't know much about Blake yet, and I've got a feeling he might be trouble. I ignored it last night, but I heard him belittling Corey's singing."

Julia nodded, her brow furrowing in thought. "Yeah, Blake's vibes are definitely off."

"But hey," Ashley added, "if things work out with you and Chris, that'll be fantastic! I'm all for it."

Julia smiled, feeling a sense of comfort in Ashley's supportive words. "Thanks, Ash. Your friendship means a lot to me."

"Always here for you," Ashley replied, giving her a reassuring hug.

***

The barn was dimly lit, the smell of hay and leather hanging in the air as Chris gave his horse a little extra attention. As he brushed the horse's flank, the stable's wooden doors swung open, and Pete, Chase, and Blake stomped in, their boots echoing on the hard-packed dirt louder than the hooves of the horses they were leading in.

Chris looked up and greeted them with a nod. "How'd the range treat you today?"

Pete shrugged, telltale exhaustion in his eyes. "Same as always. Chase and I rounded up a few strays, but it took longer than we thought."

Chase chimed in with a grin. "Yeah, those little devils can be sneaky."

Blake, seemingly less fatigued than the others, quickly finished unsaddling his horse. He slung the saddle over the rail, headed for the exit, and left without a word to Chris.

Chris, seizing the opportunity, cleared his throat and addressed his companions. "Hey, fellas, I wanted to talk to you about Blake."

Pete and Chase exchanged glances, their expressions wary. Chris hesitated for a moment, choosing his words carefully. "I noticed something strange today. Blake wasn't with you the whole time you were on the range. He came into town."

Pete's eyebrows shot up, a frown creasing his brow. "What was he doing in town?"

Chris shook his head. "I'm not sure. He said he was getting coffee for you."

"No way."

"I didn't think so. But it got me thinking. Maybe we should keep an eye on him. He's new here, and I don't want any trouble."

Chase considered the suggestion, his gaze thoughtful. "Well, he did a good job rounding up those strays today, but he sure was out of our sight a long time to do it. Now I know why."

Pete rubbed his chin, deep in thought. "Yeah, but we can't ignore this. That was an out-and-out lie. And leaving us without a word … well, that could end up being dangerous."

Chris nodded, his mind made up. "I'll keep watching him this week. Then, next weekend, I'll talk to Jet and Martha about him."

Pete and Chase exchanged another look, this one more resolute. "Sounds like a plan," Pete agreed.

With their decision made, the three cowboys returned to their tasks, the conversation hanging in the air like a lingering storm cloud. They might not know what to expect from Blake, but they were determined to protect the ranch.

Chapter 9

THE CLASSROOM QUICKLY emptied as students filed out after the final bell. Julia's jaw was clenched and she had to make an effort to loosen it and say goodbye to a couple of girls who offered sympathetic smiles. As soon as the last one left, she closed her classroom door, turned off the lights, and sat at her desk. She pulled out her phone, her thoughts anchored on the day's challenges and especially this last class with its defiant juniors. With a sigh, she began to type a message to her anonymous mentor.

HEY THERE, NEED TO VENT. 2 BOYS WERE SO BELLIGERENT AND DISRESPECTFUL TODAY THAT I'M THINKING OF QUITTING.

After a few minutes, her phone buzzed with a reply.

BUT YOU LOVE TEACHING. DON'T QUIT. TRY A 1 ON 1 TALK FIRST. THERE MIGHT BE UNDERLYING ISSUES CAUSING BAD BEHAVIOR.

Julia contemplated his suggestion, considering the complexity of her students' lives.

THANKS FOR THE SUGGESTION. GOOD IDEA. MAYBE THERE'S SOMETHING GOING ON I'M NOT AWARE OF. I MIGHT ASK THEIR COUNSELOR FIRST.

As she waited for a response, she wondered about this person. Before she'd imagined the anonymous texter to be a fatherly figure, but now she preferred to put a cowboy hat on her mental image. She chuckled to herself and thought she might ask the ranch hands a few questions at supper tonight. They were all teenage boys once and perhaps their advice might be insightful. A moment later she got another response.

ARE THEY IN SPORTS? A COACH CAN MAKE SUBTLE SUGGESTIONS OR THREATS.

Julia raised an eyebrow at that. It was a good idea. Her phone pinged again.

DON'T QUIT TEACHING. WHAT WOULD YOU DO INSTEAD?

She looked out the window and thought about the question. What would she do? Her friend Ashley had had a good job at a bank and gave it up to teach riding at the Double Horseshoe Ranch. And Dawn had been fired from her office job before coming to the ranch as a cook. Could she make that kind of radical change, too?

She sighed. She loved her students. Most of them. She loved teaching. She liked making lessons and quizzes and tests and projects. She liked grading papers and going to meetings and conducting parent-teacher conferences. She was good at explaining things.

She started tapping out a response: I DON'T KNOW. REAL ESTATE MAYBE? OR CATTLE HERDING. LOL

That was silly and she knew it. She'd picked two things farthest from the profession she knew she'd never give up. She smiled to herself, the quiet of the empty school building settling around her.

CATTLE HERDING? ARE YOU OUT WEST?

Her fingers hovered over the screen as she considered how to answer. She hadn't given much personal information to this person. Maybe it was time to … no, this could be some scammer overseas, waiting for the opportunity to get friendlier before asking for money.

Her fingers danced over the screen as she composed a message to her anonymous mentor.

SORRY, I'M NOT COMFORTABLE SAYING.

The screen pulsed and then she got a long answer.

SORRY. I PROMISE I'M NOT A STALKER OR ANYTHING. I PROMISE I'M A GOOD GUY. YOU KNOW, THE KIND WHO WEARS A WHITE HAT. SAVES THE DAY. RIDES OFF INTO THE SUNSET.

Julia considered this a moment. Her mental image of him got a whole lot closer to fitting in with the cowboys at the ranch.

OKAY. WELL, IF YOUR ADVICE WORKS, I'LL GET YOU A HORSE AND A WHITE HAT.

He responded and the texting continued in a more humorous vein. Julia felt her earlier tension relaxing. She rather enjoyed when Mr. Anonymous cheered her up like this. It occurred to her that she could search his phone number online and maybe get some information about him: what state he was in, a name, an age. She started typing into her school computer then shook her head. She didn't want to be one of those women who fell for a non-existent online illusion and tracking him felt unethical.

She packed up her bag with the papers she had to correct tonight and headed out.

Later, the warmth of the ranch house and the aroma of Dawn's hearty cooking encircled Julia as she sat at the dining room table. The ranch hands came in as a group, snowflakes still clinging to their coats as the weather couldn't make up its mind, sending wet drops then fat flakes.

Ashley and Martha exchanged stories about their day spent teaching riders how to manage their horses on the snowy trails. Martha made known her excitement for the upcoming construction of the indoor arena.

"I can't wait for it," she said. "It's going to be such a game-changer for the riding school."

Chris, sitting across from Julia, said, "Yeah, the crew is set to start in a few days. It'll be up in no time. They told me a pole barn of that size would only take seven working days to erect." Then he turned his attention to Julia and asked with genuine interest, "So, teacher-lady, how did your day go?"

Julia let out a sigh, her frustrations from earlier bubbling up. "Well," she looked around the table at faces eager to hear something different than horses or cattle stories, "I had a bit of a tough day. In my last class, there were these two students who were just ... awful. Belligerent, disrespectful, you name it."

"Boys?" Dawn asked.

"Of course."

Pete, chewing a mouthful of food, nodded and suggested, "You oughta get an administrator in there, show 'em who's boss."

"Yeah," Sawyer swallowed what he was chewing and added, "or find out who their girlfriends are. Sometimes, girls can get a guy to straighten up real quick."

Corey smiled at Ashley and said, "Yeah, find out who their girlfriends are, that'll definitely give you some leverage."

Blake tapped his fork against his plate and interrupted with a smirk, "Or I could just rough 'em up a bit." That didn't earn him the response he expected.

Martha, her manner more sympathetic, advised Julia, "Here's what you do, dear, you should call their parents. Sometimes that's all it takes."

Before Julia could react, Chris spoke up, his voice confident and convincing, "I think you might get better results if you catch each of them outside the classroom tomorrow and quietly ask for their cooperation."

Julia's eyes widened with surprise. The similarity between Chris's advice and that of her anonymous mentor sent a shiver down her spine. She couldn't help but wonder if there was more to this cowboy than met the eye. She started nodding her head in agreement. "Thanks, everyone, I'll try all your suggestions ... but I think I'll start with Chris's. Thanks Chris."

That evening Julia sat in the cozy living room of the ranch house, engrossed in correcting her students' papers, the faint glow of the television casting a soft light. Martha, absorbed in her favorite TV show, occasionally glanced over at Julia as she marked papers. The atmosphere was warm and comfortable, yet Julia felt a subtle sense of awkwardness. It was odd that neither Ashley nor Dawn had stuck around after dinner.

Martha's show ended and she clicked off the set. "Julia, dear, how are you finding it here? Are you comfortable? You know, you can stay as long as you need to."

Julia looked up, red pen in hand, "Oh, it's wonderful here, Martha. Everyone has been so nice, and I'm enjoying having people around. My evenings in my apartment are so quiet and lonely. Um, I was wondering where Ashley and Dawn are."

Martha smiled. "Sorry, it's just me tonight. Ashley's in the barn with Corey; they took Duke with them. You know, they often escape there to spend some private moments. It seems that's their regular rendezvous habit now. And Dawn and Jet went to meet with the pastor to discuss their wedding." She glanced at the door. "Sometimes one or two of the guys come over to watch with me. I guess they've got something else to do tonight."

Julia put a grade on a paper and started on a new one.

"You know," Martha kept talking, "I'm surprised Chris didn't stay. I've noticed his interest in you."

Julia shifted in her chair, her papers momentarily forgotten. "Well, to tell you the truth, I ... I'm kind of interested in him." She felt her cheeks getting warm, but talking about her feelings with the older woman was easier than doing so with her own mother. Martha's gray hair marked her as old, but her spirit was young.

Before Martha could respond, they heard the side door slam, and a moment later Ashley burst into the room, her face flushed with distress, her eyes full of tears, Duke trotting after her. Without a word, she rushed off to her room, leaving Julia and Martha intrigued and concerned.

"I'll go see what's the matter." Julia set her papers on the side table and hurried down the hall.

She entered Ashley's room, and found her friend sitting on the edge of the bed, blubbering like a baby, the dog trying to lick her face.

"Ashley, Ashley, what happened? You didn't break up with Corey, did you?"

Ashley shook her head, her shoulders slumping as she recounted the argument. "Not yet, but we had a huge fight. I wanted to spend more time with him, but he's been so busy lately. He says he wants to be with me, but his actions don't match his words. It's like he's pulling away. All he wants to do is write songs."

"I thought you two were doing that together."

"We were, but … I don't know. I don't know what to do at this point, Jules. I'm frustrated and confused." She buried her face in Duke's neck and rubbed his fur.

"Well, how about this? You know I have this anonymous mentor who's been helping me with advice. He's been surprisingly insightful. What if I text him and see if he has any guidance for you?"

"Are you even sure it's a guy?"

"Pretty sure."

"Okay," she let go of Duke and he lay down by the door, "but be specific. Tell him Corey's a cowboy and a songwriter and he sings in a bar one or two nights a week and … and … his girlfriend, me, only wants a couple of hours in the evenings. How do I get a stubborn cowboy to do that?"

Julia nodded and quickly sent a text message to her mentor, explaining the situation.

As they waited for a response, Ashley recounted Corey's exact words.

Chapter 10

CHRIS SAT AROUND the worn card table with Pete, Chase, and Matt, the hundred-watt bulb of the bunkhouse's overhead light illuminating the straight flush Pete had just laid down. They were voicing their disgust at his good luck at poker when the door swung open and Corey stormed in, his face red with frustration and exasperation.

"I swear, women can be downright impossible sometimes." He put his coat on a peg and picked up the instrument he'd left on the couch.

He slumped into a nearby chair, his fingers immediately finding the comforting strings of his guitar. He plucked at them, creating a somber melody.

The guys continued with their poker game as Corey added a few mumbled lyrics. Four hands of poker later and all four guys got bored of the game. Chase threw his cards down and took out a package of Life Savers. He popped one out with his thumbnail, set it on his tongue, then stomped off to his room. The other three turned their attention to their phones; Chris stared at the lengthy text from Julia, reread it, and looked intently at Corey.

"You know, Corey, sometimes a man doesn't need to say a word for someone to see what's eating at him. You got something on your mind, and I'm pretty sure I can guess what it is."

Pete and Matt glanced up from their phones as Chris rose and went to sit across from Corey.

Corey grunted and strummed another chord.

Chris's voice took on a sage-like tone as he seemingly divined Corey's woes. "You're feeling like you haven't had enough time to work on your songs, but working on your songs has been getting in the way of the woman you care about. And you had a spat with Ashley because she wants more of your time, right?" He knew he was right; he had Julia's text to prove it though he'd never reveal that secret.

Corey's eyes widened, and he set his guitar aside, his frustration giving way to amazement. "How the hell did you know all that?"

Chris grinned and gave Corey a knowing look.

"Well, it's part of my cowboy magic, my friend. Now, here's what you need to do." Chris laid out his advice, urging him to take action tonight.

Corey jumped up, pulled out his truck keys, swung an arm through his jacket, and left.

The other cowboys exchanged impressed glances.

Pete said, "I've never seen someone read a man like that."

Chase nodded. "That's some next-level cowboy wisdom right there."

Pete chuckled: "Well, if Chris says he knows what's going on, you better believe it."

Chris reached for his phone, typing out a text to Julia: TELL HER TO FIX HER MAKE-UP AND EXPECT A VISIT. YOUR

FRIEND'S BOYFRIEND SHOULD BE SHOWING UP WITH
FLOWERS SOON, OR HE'S NOT A REAL COWBOY.

He pressed send, a satisfied smile on his face.

***

Julia read the text aloud to Ashley. "It's not exactly
advice, but ... well, we'll see if it's prophetic. Dry your tears,
fix your face, and let's sit out in the living room and wait.
Maybe Corey will come and apologize."

Ashley raised her eyebrows. "You're serious? This guy
you don't know sends you a text and you think we should
believe it? I cannot imagine Corey going out now and finding
flowers. It's after eight, nothing's going to be open."

Julia gave her a look. "Just come on. Sit with Martha and
me. You can chat with her as I finish up my work."

Ashley checked her face in the mirror. "All right." She
cleaned off some smudged mascara. "But I'm not going to
waste my time getting gorgeous for a no-show."

Julia stood next to her and checked her own reflection in
the mirror. She had to admit to herself that she had freshened
up her own make-up before dinner so she'd look nice for
Chris.

They went out to the living room, followed by Duke, and
Ashley told Martha a shortened version of the argument. Julia
went back to grading papers and Martha and Ashley
discussed the riding classes they were teaching.

After a while, Julia texted her mysterious phone buddy.
ARE YOU SURE?

She immediately got a response: I PROMISE.

It was after nine o'clock when headlights swept the front
window and a door slammed. Duke raised his head, then set
it back down on his paws. A moment later a timid knock
preceded the opening of the front door. Corey entered, sighed

when he saw there'd be witnesses, and held out a bouquet of flowers.

"I'm sorry, Ashley. These are for you. My apologies. Twelve of them. Yellow roses."

Ashley leaped up and threw her arms around his neck. Martha and Julia sneaked out of the room.

As she got to her bedroom Julia texted YOU WERE RIGHT. I GUESS YOU KNOW COWBOYS.

The answer came quickly: I AM ONE.

Chapter 11

THE BITTER WIND sliced through the open expanse of the range, chilling the cowboys to their bones as they rode in search of some missing cattle. A cold silence hung in the air as the snow-laden landscape stretched out before them. Chris, Corey, Blake, Pete, Matt, and Sawyer were already used to battling the unforgiving elements, their horses steadfast against the biting cold. The search had been difficult, and they had only managed to locate half the herd.

The guys rode in a loose formation, their eyes scanning the horizon for any sign of the wayward herd. The first traces of sunlight painted the sky a pale pink, offering a glimmer of warmth in the frigid morning.

Sawyer, always quick with a jest, broke the silence, attempting to lighten the mood. "Maybe those stray cattle went to town to buy flowers for their sweethearts." He aimed a smirk at Corey.

Corey shot back with a grin, "At least I have a sweetheart to buy flowers for."

Snorts of laughter punched through the early morning quiet, but the worry about the cattle kept everyone on edge. Matt and Pete took off in one direction to scout over the ridge, and Chris sent Corey and Sawyer to go toward the little lake. Chris, now alone with Blake and a few dozen cattle, decided to confront Blake about his dishonesty, suspecting it had a connection to their missing cattle.

He flipped his coat collar up around his neck, his breath visible in the chilly air, and turned in his saddle to Blake, his eyes sharp with determination.

"Blake, something's not right. The other day you left the herd, came to town with some half-baked story that Pete sent you for coffee. I thought you were following Julia, but now I'm thinking you were up to something else. We're missing half the herd. I can't shake the feeling that you have something to do with that."

Blake, his face turning slightly red, tried to brush it off. "Hah, that's a laugh. What? You think I'm in with some cattle rustlers or something?"

"That's exactly what I'm thinking."

"I ain't stupid. Why would I do that the first week I'm here? If I were a cow thief I'd settle in for months before pullin' a stunt like that. Avoid suspicion." He huffed and reined his horse closer. "This is just a coincidence. Hasn't your ranch been hit before?"

Chris shook his head slowly. He leaned in closer, his voice low and intense. "We're a team out here. If you've got any idea what's happened to the herd, you need to speak up."

Blake, his face reddening even more, shifted in his saddle. His quick anger bubbled to the surface. "You think you know everything, huh? Maybe I should teach you a lesson or two, cowboy."

He looked ready to leap off his horse, ready to let his fists do the talking, but Chris held his gaze, unyielding and firm.

"This isn't about fighting, Blake. It's about honesty and responsibility. I don't want to call you a flannel-mouthed liar, but …"

The tense silence hung in the air, the wind carrying his last word away. Blake sat back in his saddle. "All right, maybe I've been less than truthful. But I got my reasons. I'll come clean soon, I promise."

Chris nodded, "Fair enough. But remember, we're in this together. Let's find those cattle and head back before this weather gets the better of us."

***

Before her last class of the day, Julia stood in the hallway by her door and snagged one of the boys who'd given her a rough time the day before.

"Hey, Liam," she said with a tentative smile, "can I ask you for a favor?" Without waiting for a response, she dove right in. "The other kids in class seem to look up to you and Tanner. Um, I have a particularly frustrating lesson to get through today. I was hoping you guys could keep everyone on track today. You know, ask good questions, shush the losers who groan," her smile got real, "and, uh, make me look good." She laughed and so did Liam.

"Yeah, sure." He walked on and into the room, a somewhat pleasant but confused look on his face.

A moment later, his buddy Tanner sauntered down the hall toward the room, calling out loudly to a pair of girls going the other way. He caught sight of Julia and his face drooped a bit.

"Hey, Ms. Brown. Sorry about yesterday."

"Thanks for the apology, Tanner." She gave him her most disarming smile. "That's very mature of you." She leaned a tad closer and lowered her voice. "You're actually one of my

60

most promising students. I was hoping you'd help me keep Liam and the others engaged in today's lesson. Do you think you could do that?"

His eyebrows knitted together and he asked, "What can *I* do?"

"For one, you can keep that charming smile of yours ready. I've noticed the girls watching you. Did you know they look away when you say stuff like you did yesterday? But they're quite taken with you when you smile and ask smart questions."

"Oh, uh, okay. I can do that."

***

Dinner at the ranch that night was quieter than usual if you can call only three people talking at the same time instead of eight or nine quieter.

Dawn and Jet chatted with Martha about their visit with the pastor, telling her the relationship exercises he'd assigned them to complete before their next meeting.

Ashley and Corey argued gently over one line of a new song he was writing and Pete and Matt related their difficulties rounding up some of the cattle. Sawyer asked Chris when he thought the little lake would freeze over and Chris, helping himself to seconds of the baked chicken, said it might skim over with thin ice well before Christmas.

"Hey," Blake, farther down the table from Julia tonight, yelled, "teacher-lady, did you get those slackers to toe the line today?"

Julia set down her fork and nodded. "It was Chris's advice that worked. I talked to each kid before he entered the class. No discipline necessary. They were model students today. I only hope it lasts."

Blake's face, which had darkened when she credited Chris, now shifted into a devilish smirk. "I'm not surprised. I had a hot teacher like you when I was in school. I'd've done anything to get into her pants, too."

The hush that fell over the table was instant. Chris rose from his chair, his intention to yank Blake out of his seat and throw him out of the house more than evident by his growl and his own chair falling back.

Martha rose, too. "Chris. Sit down. Blake, please apologize to our guest. I don't know how they talk to women where you come from, but you will be more respectful when you're in my house."

All eyes were on her. It was unheard of for Martha to raise her voice, let alone speak in any tone other than sweet.

Blake's smirk was replaced by a whistle through tight lips. "Whew. Didn't mean nothin' by that, ma'am. Sorry, Ms. Julia." He stuffed a roll in his mouth and started chewing, but there was a glint of defiance in the look he sent Chris.

Chris, seated again, said, "Great dinner, Dawn, as usual." He avoided looking at Julia.

Ashley tried to lighten the mood. "Hey, everyone, I helped Dawn with dessert this afternoon. You're going to love it. Chocolate cake with penuche frosting."

That started the conversations again as several of the guys had never heard of penuche.

Julia kept glancing at Chris until finally their eyes met and she mouthed a silent 'thank you.'

Chapter 12

THE AIR IN the barn was thick with the scent of leather, hay, and the comforting aroma of horses as Chris walked in and headed toward the stable office to speak with Jet and Martha. He could hear their excited voices as they discussed the logistics of the upcoming construction. He reached the half-open door. Jet and Martha were bent over Martha's worn, cluttered desk, examining the blueprint plans and the paperwork for the pole barn. The anticipation of the new addition to the ranch was tangible, but a pressing issue weighed on Chris's mind and he had to interrupt them.

He knocked lightly and pushed open the creaky door the rest of the way, his boots thudding against the wooden floor. His face cued concern and urgency.

"Jet, Martha, we got a wolf problem on our hands. Signs of them are everywhere. And, well, Sawyer called in from the range … they found the remains of a calf the wolves feasted on last night."

Martha looked up, her brow furrowing as alarm etched lines into her face. Jet's eyes narrowed, his rugged features reflecting the gravity of the situation.

"Wolves?" Martha breathed. "On Double Horseshoe land?"

"Yup, it's not normal, I know. But there's been a sudden surge across the state. Missing cattle, pets, chickens. I've seen tracks all around. Probably that's why the herd got split in half the other day."

Jet let out an exasperated breath. "Dang it all. We can't afford to lose more head of cattle, especially not now."

Chris nodded, his hat pulled low against his forehead. He lifted it and ran a hand through his hat-flattened hair, frustrated but determined. "I suppose it might be one of those rare migrations, and they're only passing through. Something's throwing them off their usual patterns."

Martha placed a comforting hand on Chris's arm, her concern evident. "We'll need to be vigilant. Keep a sharp eye out."

"Right, I'll double up patrols. We'll take turns pulling all-nighters."

Jet's eyes focused on the blueprint, deep in thought. He shook his head and then looked Chris in the eye. "Make sure all the cowhands are armed. We don't want to take chances."

"Right." Chris tipped his hat and strode out.

In the stable office, Martha and Jet exchanged glances.

"I think we should tell the girls. I don't want them going out riding alone. Packs tend to stick to their territories. But this ... this feels different." He snorted. "Heck, even walking to the barn might be dangerous."

Martha tucked a strand of gray hair behind one ear. "We can use Duke as an escort."

***

Inside Brew Haven café, the aroma of freshly brewed coffee filled the air as Julia sat at a cozy table with her friends, Emma and Megan. They had gathered for their regular catch-up session, sharing laughs and heart-to-heart conversations, and gossiping about the romance that was keeping Ashley away from them this time.

Julia stirred her coffee, the cup cradled between her hands as she shared tidbits of her life at the Double Horseshoe Ranch. Emma and Megan leaned in, engrossed in her tales.

Julia's face lit up as she related her unique living situation. "It's incredible, really. I've never been around so many cowboys in my life. Each one of them is like a character from a Western movie, and the ranch itself is like something out of a storybook."

Megan chuckled, her eyes dancing with expectation. "Full make-up on for breakfast?"

"Of course. Half the guys come in early, scarf down Dawn's eggs and bacon—some mornings there are cinnamon rolls—and then they gallop off to the range. A couple are there when I eat and whoever's left must come in after I leave for school."

Megan nearly drooled. "A parade of men. How wonderful. What about the evenings?"

Julia's cheeks turned a delicate shade of pink, and she hesitated for a moment before replying. "Well, that's the best time. We all sit down together. Like a family. Six-thirty sharp. At first, most of them looked scruffy. You know, tired and dirty from being on a horse all day, but lately I think they're rushing to shower and show up looking pretty hot."

"For your benefit." Emma nodded her head, grinning. "You are so lucky. Who's the hottest? I mean, I've seen them all either at the rodeo or at the Circle Bar or around town, but not up close."

"There is one in particular."

Emma leaned in closer, her voice tinged with excitement. "Yeah? The one you were drooling over at the rodeo?"

Julia's gaze wandered toward the window, her thoughts drifting to Chris Thornton, the rugged cowboy who had captured her attention weeks ago. Just thinking about him put her heart into a hard cantering rhythm. "Mm-hmm. His name's Chris. He's got this serious charm, and he's always there with a kind word or a helpful gesture. He's given me good advice."

"Describe him."

"Hazel eyes, three-day beard, and a warmth that draws people in. He's ... I guess you'd call him the foreman ... he's in charge of the other cowboys. Chris is ... something else. He's kind, and hardworking, and he really cares about the ranch. He's got a genuine way about him."

Megan and Emma exchanged knowing glances, their smiles widening. It was clear to them that Julia was smitten with this cowboy.

Megan said, "Well, you know, Christmas is just around the corner, and I happen to be hosting an early Christmas party at my townhouse. I've booked the communal room in the clubhouse. Why don't you ask Chris to be your date?"

Julia's eyes widened at the suggestion. She had been wondering how to get their relationship to move on to something other than riding to church with him, but the idea of asking Chris to a party was a leap she wasn't sure she was ready to make. She took a sip of her coffee, her mind racing.

"I'll think about it. I wouldn't want to be too forward ... to impose or make things awkward."

Emma offered a reassuring smile. "Impose? It's the twenty-first century. Women can take the lead."

As they continued to chat, Julia enjoyed the quiver of excitement at the thought of the upcoming Christmas party. Maybe, just maybe, it was time to take a chance on the handsome cowboy who made her heart flutter every time she saw him.

***

Julia was disappointed at supper when three of the cowboys weren't there; Chris was one of them.

Jet explained, "Chris, Blake, and Matt are out with the herd tonight. We've got a problem with wolves."

Ashley, Dawn, and Julia reacted with surprise. Martha nodded briskly. "Don't go outside at night alone. Wolves are generally afraid of humans and the risk of them attacking one of us is low, but … be aware of your surroundings."

 The rest of the meal was eaten with less enthusiasm as the conversation stayed serious and each one contemplated the implications.

Later, in Ashley's room, Julia and Ashley talked of happier things. Ashley's relationship with Corey was back on track and Julia relayed Megan and Emma's updates: Megan's boyfriend was still out of town and Emma's was still acting like a jerk. They'd broken up again.

Julia glanced often at the flowers on her dresser. "Are you and Corey going to Megan's party?"

"We sure are. Corey's been warming up on Christmas tunes, in case she asks him to bring his guitar."

"Mm. I was talking with Megan and Emma about the party. I was sort of thinking of asking Chris to go with me."

Ashley clapped her hands together. "About time you made a move. Have you noticed how he looks at you?"

"I have. But he hasn't asked me out yet, well, other than for a sandwich after church. I'm afraid that my apartment will be fixed soon and I won't be seeing him here every day. Out of sight, out of mind. He'll forget about me."

Ashley reached over and plucked one of the flowers from the vase and held the petals to her nose. "Actually … I was wondering if one or two of the other guys might ask you out this weekend. Would you consider going out with … uh … Pete?"

"Pete?" Julia watched Ashley run her fingers down the stem and flick a drop of water off the end. She squinted her eyes at Ashley. "Did he say something to Corey?"

"Sort of. Corey told me that you are a hot topic in the bunkhouse. It was obvious at first that Blake might be in to you, but that's cooled down. I think because one of the other guys has quelled his interest. Maybe told him to back off. It might have been Chris or Pete."

Julia didn't speak for the moments it took for her to wrap her head around the possibility of Pete. The guy, though maybe a little older, was every bit as good-looking, well-mannered, and polite as Chris. He was more the quiet type, but still … she shook her head. "No, Pete seems nice and all, but I don't think I'd go out with him if he asked."

"Good to know. I'll pass that on to Corey and he can warn Pete so he doesn't embarrass himself."

Julia chuckled. "I'll be the one embarrassing myself if I ask Chris to this party."

"Why don't you get some advice from your secret mentor?"

"Ha!" Julia pulled her phone out of her pocket. "That would be interesting." She scrolled through her texts. "I haven't heard from him today. Did I tell you he admitted to being a cowboy?"

"No way."

"Okay, here goes. I'm going to do it." She read her question aloud to Ashley as she typed: "HEY, THERE'S A

COWBOY I LIKE HERE. ANY ADVICE ON HOW TO ROPE HIM IN?"

Ashley howled with laughter. "Send it."

Julia, her heart aflutter with anticipation, glanced at her phone as a message from her anonymous mentor flashed on the screen only a few moments later.

"WELL, DARLING, YOU'VE GOT THE LASSO OF YOUR CHARM. NOW, JUST BE YOURSELF AND LET THE COWBOY WANDER RIGHT INTO IT. 😊 "

Ashley bounced on the bed. "He sounds awesome. You've got to find out where he lives and who he is."

"Probably some old guy. I'm not going to waste my time when there's a real man right here."

"Okay, then. Well, it looks like your mentor has given you the green light. You can ask Chris. Go get him, cowgirl!"

"Not so fast. I'm going to ask one more thing." Her fingers tapped away and then she read what she wrote: "I WANT TO ASK HIM TO A PARTY. SHOULD I WAIT UNTIL HE ASKS ME OUT FIRST?"

A few moments later the answer came back: "YES."

"Oh ... well ... I wasn't expecting that."

Ashley put the rose back and said, "So ... there's time yet. Maybe he'll ask you out this weekend."

"Or maybe not, with all these night shifts they're riding ... I'm not getting my hopes up. Megan's party is a week and a half away. I guess I'll be going alone."

"You can ride with me and Corey."

Chapter 13

C HRIS SAT ON his bunk, his thumb hovering over his phone screen, a small smirk playing on his lips. He couldn't help but chuckle at his last text to Julia. It was true; he needed to ask her out soon. A sense of exhilaration coursed through him. A chance like this didn't come around every day. But what would she enjoy doing? His hazel eyes glinted as he speculated, the warmth of his room doing little to thaw the chill in his bones from the long day on the range.

As the winter wind howled outside, swirling snowflakes danced by his window. The thought of her had become a gentle blaze in his thoughts, warming him despite the cold Montana night.

Should I ask her out now? Chris pondered, a swirl of nervous excitement building within. He knew he had to seize the moment, yet he was unsure of the kind of date that would resonate with Julia. His mind wandered, envisioning shared laughter and meaningful conversations against a backdrop of starlit skies.

With a sudden resolve, Chris decided to seek advice from his bunkmates. With a deep breath, Chris pushed the door open and strolled into the main area of the bunkhouse, where the other cowboys were gathered. The room was dimly lit, and the air was filled with the earthy scent of leather, sweat, and fresh coffee.

He cleared his throat, breaking the jovial chatter that filled the air.

"Hey, fellas, what do you all do for fun around here? I mean ... you know, with ... women," Chris asked, attempting a nonchalant tone that concealed the burgeoning butterflies in his stomach.

Sawyer, who was sharpening a knife, glanced up briefly. "Not much, Chris. Just the usual–hitting the bar, catching a movie, or grabbing a bite to eat in town."

Blake, sprawled out on the couch, yawned noisily. "Yeah, not much to do around here."

Pete furrowed his brows, suspicion lacing his tone. "Why're you asking, Chris? You planning on taking someone out?"

Catching the look in Pete's eyes, Chris stumbled over his own words, attempting to steer the conversation away from his newfound interest. "Oh, you know ... bored ... looking for things to do. Not everything has to revolve around work."

Sawyer looked up, "Well, you could go to the Circle Bar, catch some live music. Corey's singing again. Or there's a new movie in town."

Chase nodded in agreement, adding, "Maybe a nice dinner at that restaurant across from the Brew Haven."

Throughout the suggestions, Pete's gaze remained fixated on Chris. "Yeah, but what if you're thinking about someone special, someone like ... Julia? Those ideas won't work for a college grad like her, will they?"

Chris scratched his jaw, trying to play it cool, but his mind raced. "Well, I don't know. Just looking for ideas."

Chris felt the weight of Pete's words settle on his shoulders, the truth undeniable. There was a tension in the room, a silent understanding that maybe they were both interested in the same woman. A gentle conflict swirled beneath the surface, leaving Chris to grapple with his emotions. He would have expected some pushback from Blake, but he'd never considered Pete might be interested in Julia.

Pete's dark eyes bore into Chris, an unspoken challenge between them. "Who's the lucky lady you got in mind?"

"I'd rather not say … it's someone I've been texting for weeks now." He watched Pete's face look relieved. That wasn't good.

***

The cold night air carried a hushed urgency as Chris hurried back to the ranch house, the quiet crunch of snow under his boots echoing his determined pace. His heart drummed a wild beat in his chest, the prospect of asking Julia out fueling his steps. He knew he had to seize this chance, to unravel the possibilities that seemed to dance in the frosty air.

The night was veiled in a frigid shroud and strange sounds. He scanned the area, remembering the threat of wolves. He thought he saw a dark shape moving near the barn. Probably Duke, he thought as he continued to stride purposefully toward the ranch house. He was excited to see Julia.

As he approached the ranch house, his heart quickened its pace, anticipation mingling with trepidation. He could already envision the warmth of her smile, the sparkle in her eyes, as he posed the question that had been occupying his thoughts when he was on the range. The porch light spilled a soft, inviting glow onto the frozen ground, a beacon drawing him closer.

But as he neared the door, it swung open with a sudden burst of energy, and Martha's voice rang out, summoning her dog. "Duke, come on boy, get inside!" For a moment, the anticipation waned, replaced by confusion as he looked back toward the barn. Duke was nowhere in sight.

"Hey, Martha, I just saw him." He changed course from the side door to bounding up the steps to the front porch, waving in the direction of the stable.

Martha came all the way out, her arms wrapped around herself, and hollered again. "Duke! Come on, Duke!" She looked at Chris. "You don't think he's out running with the wolves, do you? I let him out an hour ago." He shrugged and she added, "I'll bet you're back for seconds on Dawn's apple pie."

Then, he heard it—an anguished whimper, a sound that tugged at his heartstrings. He turned, his eyes searching the surrounding darkness, and there, huddled against the biting cold at the side of the house, was Duke. The dog's normally robust form now appeared forlorn, injured.

"Holy smokes, Martha. I think he's hurt." He rushed back down the steps and went to him. His eyes darted back toward the barn, realizing he'd not seen Duke there a moment ago, but rather a wolf.

Chris knelt beside the wounded canine, his fingers gently probing Duke's body and finding a sticky wet warmth. It was clear that Duke had tangled with that wolf and it hadn't gone well.

"Martha, go inside. I'll take him to the vet," Chris said softly, his voice filled with quiet strength.

As Martha withdrew, her lamentations limited to simple words—"Oh no, oh no"—the porch was repopulated with Ashley and Julia who wanted to see what the commotion was.

"Oh, poor Duke," they both cried as one. Chris lifted Duke gently in his arms, the German Shepherd whimpering.

Julia, her eyes filled with empathy, asked, "Do you need any help?"

The offer was a lifeline. "Yes," Chris replied. "If you wouldn't mind coming along. I'm not exactly sure where the vet clinic is."

"I'll grab my coat."

***

The sterile, fluorescent-lit waiting room of the veterinary clinic enveloped Julia and Chris in a cocoon of tension and worry. The uncomfortable plastic chairs creaked beneath them as they sat side by side, sharing silent moments of apprehension. Their eyes spoke volumes, mirroring the unspoken concern so clearly revealed on their faces.

Julia's fingers clenched and unclenched nervously in her lap. She was anguished for the dog but also desperate to ask Chris a particular question. Her gaze drifted toward him often, finding more to admire about him. His eyes, those enigmatic hazel orbs, stayed focused on the door to the examination room and his fingers kept rotating the edges of the credit card he'd used to pay for whatever was necessary.

"He'll be all right," she whispered to him.

"I hope so. Martha's had him since he was a pup. Got him after her husband died." He pulled out his wallet and inserted the card.

Julia sucked in a whole lungful of air and sighed it out through her nose. "It's hard losing a pet. I had a dog once.

When he died … that was the most crying I've ever done in my life."

"Yeah," Chris put his hand on hers, "same here."

"What if the doctor has to put him down?"

Chris lifted his hand from hers and said, "That's not going to happen. Duke's strong. He can recover. They're only bites."

"Wolf bites." She shook her head and bit her lips. "Duke was the friendliest welcome I got when I came to Double Horseshoe."

Chris huffed a laugh. "Aw, come on, all of us cowboys were friendly, weren't we?"

Their conversation ebbed and flowed like a gentle tide, shifting from their shared worry about Duke's condition to faintly flirty joking.

The veterinarian's sudden appearance brought them both to their feet, and they focused in as if to absorb every word. The news was a mixed bag; relief and concern mingled in the explanation and instructions. Duke had several bites needing stitching and while he would recover, the road to his full health might be a trying one.

"I'd like to keep him overnight," the vet said, "and then you'll have to watch him for signs of rabies. I'll give you a pamphlet on it. Unfortunately, there's no test to diagnose infection. My records show he was vaccinated against it as a pup, but he hasn't been back to receive a re-vaccination since." He raised his eyebrows. "Montana doesn't have a statewide requirement, but it's recommended."

Chris gave a nod. "I'll tell Martha."

Leaving the sterile clinic behind, they stepped out into the crisp winter air. Chris held the door for Julia and she climbed up into the truck's cab easily. Chris started the engine as soon as he got in. It hummed softly, the heater coming on quickly, a soothing contrast to the cold outside. But he didn't put it in gear.

"Martha's heart is going to shatter if Duke has rabies. She'll blame herself."

Julia felt a spurt of adrenaline charge her heart and unexpected words tumbled off her tongue in response, "You know, it couldn't hurt to pray for Duke." She interpreted Chris's look as curious surprise and not ridicule. "I mean … we've been to church together, bowed our heads—at least I did—" she lifted the corners of her mouth, "and we listened to the pastor pray. He said there was nothing too small to ask God for help about."

Chris's smile matched hers in tentativeness and shyness. "Hey, I closed my eyes." His laugh was brief. "Praying is not something I'm good at, but I've heard Martha pray at every supper since I've been here and … yeah … let's pray for Duke." He held a palm out and she set her hand in his. "But you do it."

She got another spike of something—dopamine?—but whether it was from embarrassment or fear or the physical delight of her skin on his, she wasn't sure, but she was glad she hadn't put her gloves on.

"Okay … God, please let Duke be okay and not have rabies … thank you … amen."

Chris squeezed her hand and let it go. "Not bad." He couldn't help but let a small chuckle escape, breaking the solemnity that had gripped them earlier. "So … I guess now we've advanced our, uh, relationship, to a new level." He put the truck in reverse. "Who would've thought a vet visit could count as a second date?" he mused, his eyes twinkling with a playful light. "It does count, doesn't it?"

76

Julia smiled in response, her heart dancing at the prospect of the connection they were forging. "Well, yeah, I suppose. And not a cheap date, either. Vet bills can cost a fortune."

"Tell me about it."

As they drove away from the clinic, the subject shifted to a brighter note as Chris pointed out the decorations on the stores they passed.

"I love Christmas," Julia said. "Oh, look at those lights." She *oohed* and *ahhed* as they passed a Santa and reindeer display and she found the courage to ask Chris her question. "Uh, my friend … a friend of Ashley's and mine … Megan … is having a Christmas party and I was wondering … if you'd like to go with me? It's not this Friday, but next."

Without his eyes leaving the road, Chris answered. "Yes, ma'am, I sure would. Now I have a question for you … another date … this Saturday … we can do anything you want. Anything."

Julia pressed back in her seat, more than relieved, and answered, "Absolutely anything? I accept. And I hope that credit card of yours has a high limit." She laughed. "Just kidding."

Chapter 14

JULIA WASN'T AFRAID of getting into a textual tug of war with her nameless phone friend. It was late and she should have been trying to get to sleep. She had school tomorrow and an early before-school department meeting. But she couldn't resist expressing her excitement to her mentor: HEY THERE! YOU WON'T BELIEVE WHAT HAPPENED TODAY. CHRIS ASKED ME OUT! 😀

Julia laughed aloud as she read his response: SO, AT LAST, A NAME FOR THE COWBOY. YOU SURE YOU'RE NOT TOO SOPHISTICATED FOR HIM? 😊

She typed back: YOU SAID YOU'RE A COWBOY. THEY CAN'T BE ALL BAD 😜

TRUE. SO, WHAT'S THE PLAN FOR THE BIG DATE? OR IS THIS THE XMAS PARTY?

Julia smiled. She had two dates to look forward to. She couldn't decide if she'd be more nervous about being alone with him this weekend or being in a crowd with him at a party. She was too slow in responding and a new message popped up: I THINK I'M JEALOUS OF THIS CHRIS GUY. YOU GOTTA GIVE ME SOMETHING. YOUR NAME, AT LEAST.

Julia hesitated, then typed: JULIA. AND YOU HAVE NO REASON TO BE JEALOUS. WE'LL PROBABLY NEVER MEET.

She laid the phone down and undressed for bed. She climbed in and checked her phone one last time. It read: NEVER SAY NEVER. I HAVE COWBOY POWERS. I'M GOING TO TRADE PLACES WITH THIS CHRIS. HE CAN'T POSSIBLY KNOW YOU LIKE I DO.

Julia reread it and tried not to think the texting had gotten a little out of hand. Was she misinterpreting it? This comment seemed on the verge of creepy. She decided not to answer it and set the phone down on the bedside table. She switched out the light and snuggled under the sheets and blankets.

The phone pinged. She looked. SORRY, JULIA, THAT WAS CREEPY. TELL ME WHAT YOUR FAVORITE DATE WOULD BE AND I'LL TELL YOU IF A REAL COWBOY WOULD BE UP FOR IT.

She let the message hang in the digital air for a moment. She had been worrying about that very thing. Chris was country and she was city. She'd been to college and he'd been … well, she'd never asked, but she assumed he'd been riding the range since forever.

OKAY, she typed back, I'D LIKE TO DO AN ESCAPE ROOM CHALLENGE.

She settled back onto the pillow and cradled the phone, her eyes closed. She was almost asleep when several minutes passed and an answer finally came through.

HAD TO LOOK THAT UP. SOUNDS INTERESTING BUT NOT EXACTLY 'RANCH HAND FRIENDLY.' IF HE TAKES YOU THERE, IT MEANS HE'S REALLY INTO YOU.

PROMISE?

I PROMISE. ☺

Chapter 15

THE COLD MONTANA night air seeped into the truck as Julia settled into the passenger seat, her breath forming ephemeral clouds. The dim glow of the ranch house behind them provided a serene backdrop to their third, technically first, date. Chris shut her door and moved around the front of the truck. As he slid into the driver's seat, he dropped his phone into a small cubby hole in the truck's console. He started the engine and cranked up the heat. All she noticed was the musk and spice of his cologne, filling her sense of smell with an expectation of excitement and mystery.

"Well," he said, "everybody here seems to know we're going out."

"Sorry. I told Ashley and Dawn. I'm sure they told Corey and Jet ... so they probably spilled the beans to the whole bunkhouse. Martha seemed to already know. Did the guys tease you?"

"Only Blake, and I wouldn't call it teasing. So, where would you like to go tonight?"

Julia hesitated, unsure whether to reveal her penchant for escape rooms, fearing it might seem too unconventional. Her mentor's words flashed before her eyes; the idea that she could gauge how much a guy liked her by his reaction to a quirky date seemed unlikely, but she didn't want to chance making Chris think they were too different to get along. Instead, she chose to play it cool. "I'm not picky," she replied with a faint smile. "As long as it's something we'd both enjoy. You know, like a cow-tipping, axe-throwing, or maybe staking out Big Foot," she teased.

Chris put his hand on the gear shifter and smiled. "Well," he began, and she noted a sly look on his face, "there are some cool things to do in Billings or Bozeman if you're up for a bit of a drive." He paused and his words hung in the air for a moment before he continued. "Like an amusement activity ... I've read they have ... escape rooms."

Julia's heart skipped a beat, her eyes widening in disbelief. It was as if he had plucked her secret desire right from her mind ... or from her texts.

But just as quickly as her thoughts swirled, they stilled as Chris smiled at her with a serious yet tender expression. He took his hand off the gear lever and moved his fingers as if he were about to conjure something out of thin air. "Julia, I need to tell you something."

Her heart did a little dance and she waited, trying not to breathe in the scent of his havoc-making aftershave.

"You're not going to believe this." He picked up his phone and pressed the screen.

She cocked her head ready to hear whatever it was she wasn't going to believe. But her phone pinged. The screen glowed with the same words Chris had just spoken. YOU'RE NOT GOING TO BELIEVE THIS. She looked from the text to his face and back again.

"Wait, what? How did you do that? Oh ... Ashley gave you my number?"

He shook his head. "That's not my first text to you. Scroll up ... I'm ... you'll see."

She scrolled, saw the many texts between herself and the mentor, couldn't process if he ... if Chris ... if the mentor was ... "I don't understand ... How did you ..." She looked up as he turned his phone to face her, the same series of recent texts from her nameless friend on *his* screen.

"It's me. I'm him. I'm the guy you've been asking for advice from since September."

Julia couldn't speak. Was this true? Or was it a joke? Another trick. The air in the truck had warmed, but she was downright hot. No, this wasn't a joke. It suddenly made sense. The advice ... Corey getting Ashley flowers ... the mentor practically guaranteeing he would. Her initial shock gave way to other emotions: surprise and amazement, then embarrassment and a flicker of anger.

"Why? Why didn't you tell me? When did you figure it out? Oh my gosh, you've been playing me!"

"No, no."

A storm of emotions left her irrational; she meant to reach for the door handle, but her muscles wouldn't respond. The atmosphere was abruptly more electric. Hot, very hot. Disbelief and amazement collided in waves. She might be sick. She couldn't look away from his pleading eyes. Then, before she could bring herself out of this numbness, Chris reached over and drew her closer, his lips meeting hers in a kiss that bridged the gap between paralysis and understanding.

Julia, breathless, felt the genuine warmth of his lips, tasted a sweetness that spoke of honesty. He liked her. He'd been nothing but kind and considerate and attentive and ... and she liked him. Oh, what a kiss.

The emotions swirling within her shifted again, spinning into a sense of exhilaration and joy; the uncertainty faded.

And the moment stretched. She melted into a second and third kiss, brought her fingers to his cheek and felt his arms encircle her with all that cowboy strength, tempered with restraint.

"I'm not playing you, Julia," Chris pulled back, but kept his arms around her. "I really like you and I think we've gotten to know each other through the texting better than if we just started going out tonight."

Julia still tingled from the kisses, her heart in her throat, her head a mess. "Uh-huh. It all makes sense now. Your advice about my students, about Ashley and Corey, about the Christmas party, you were dropping hints."

"I wanted to tell you right away, as soon as I figured it out, but …"

All of a sudden Julia didn't care that he'd waited; didn't care about escape rooms or dates; didn't care if the flickering porch light meant several pairs of eyes were watching and wondering why they hadn't pulled away yet. She only cared that she had the perfect guy trying his best to woo her.

"Kiss me again, cowboy, and promise me you'll …" She didn't get a chance to finish.

"I promise." Chris pulled her in for a longer, sweeter kiss than she'd ever dreamed of.

THE END

Want more?

In book 4, HEARTSTRINGS AND HORSESHOES, we get through the Montana winter with several big events including that Christmas party where something wild happens, and then there's Jet and Dawn's wedding, and … another new romance. Find the next book in the series, HEARTSTRINGS AND HORSESHOES, and find out who captures Pete's heart.

Follow me for new book releases:
https://www.amazon.com/stores/author/B003MX4NCS